COME RUNNING

Darrell Anderson had fallen in love with
Matthew Lawford, who was married –
unhappily, but married none the less. She
knew that she would still go to him on any
terms he chose to name – but was there any
chance of happiness for them, even if she did?

FOR THE LOVE OF SARA

It was over five years since Rachel and Joel had parted in anger and bitterness – and now they had met again all the old hostile feelings were there still. For Rachel was going to marry Joel's father, and Joel felt he could never forgive her. And he still didn't know her real reason for going through with this marriage . . .

COME THE VINTAGE

Ryan's father had left her a half share of his prosperous vine-growing business, and the other half to a man she had never heard of, a Frenchman named Alain de Beaunes – on condition that they married each other. So, for the sake of the business, they married, neither caring anything for the other. Where did they go from there?

TAKE WHAT YOU WANT

Sophie was only a teenager, but she knew she would never love, had never loved, anyone but her stepbrother Robert. But her whole family, including Robert, disapproved, and hoped she would get over the feeling. Were they right – or was Sophie?

DARK VENETIAN

Emma ought to have known that her stepmother Celeste never did anything except for selfish reasons, and even a holiday in a Venetian *palazzo* could not compensate her for the heart-ache she was to suffer. Celeste wanted to add a title to her wealth – but did it *have* to be Count Vidal Cesare, the man Emma herself loved?

COME RUNNING

by

ANNE MATHER

MILLS & BOON LIMITED
17-19 FOLEY STREET
LONDON WIA IDR

First published 1976
This edition 1976

© Anne Mather 1976

ISBN 0 263 71997 9

Made and Printed in Great Britain by
C. Nicholls & Company Ltd.,
The Philips Park Press, Manchester.

CHAPTER ONE

The marquee was crowded with friends and relatives all wanting to wish the happy couple every happiness, and Darrell sought the coolness of the moist air outside. It was a pity it had rained, a wet day in the small North Yorkshire town of Sedgeley was not exactly the ideal beginning to a marriage, but Susan and Frank looked so happy that Darrell had to concede that the weather meant little to them. She sighed without envy. Without that move from the London hospital to the Sedgeley Infirmary, it could well have been herself and Barry taking the plunge, but she was glad it was not. She had liked Barry well enough, she still liked him, but not enough to marry him.

She glanced back into the marquee. The toasts were over. Any minute now, Susan and Frank would be leaving for Susan's mother's house to get changed before leaving on their honeymoon. They were going to Majorca – where else? thought Darrell wryly – and then chided herself for her

5

cynicism. Susan was a nice girl, she liked her, and as fellow nurses, they worked well together.

Her heels were sinking into the damp ground beneath her feet and she looked down impatiently. The hem of her coffee-coloured gown was going to be ruined, but that couldn't be helped. No one could have expected a week of torrential rain at the beginning of June which had made the area around the marquee a veritable quagmire.

A sudden breeze brought her hand to her head to secure the wide-brimmed straw boater and with her other hand plucking the hem of her skirt out of the mud, she became aware that she was being observed with some amusement by a man standing just inside the entrance to the marquee.

She knew who the man was. She had been introduced to him earlier. He was Matthew Lawford, Susan's eldest brother, who, together with his wife, had come up from London for the wedding. But Darrell had heard about him before then. Susan talked about him a lot. She was very proud of her brother who had succeeded in getting to Oxford and was now one of the youngest financiers in the city. A tycoon, Susan called him, although Darrell suspected that was a word coined by her family and not by Matthew Lawford himself.

Her initial impressions of him were mixed. Physically, he was a very attractive man, with straight brown hair, brown eyes, and the kind of tan not associated with summers in Sedgeley. She guessed his age to be around thirty-two or thirty-three, and although his beginnings were not in doubt, several years living in London had smoothed out most of his accent. He was tall, without an ounce of superfluous flesh on his bones, and his clothes, obviously out of the class of those of his father and brothers, fitted him with ease and elegance. And yet elegant wasn't a word Darrell would have used to describe him. His face was too hard for that, his manner occasionally exhibiting a toughness which would not be out of place in the wrestling ring. It was the sinuous way he moved that drew attention to his appearance, a kind of grace simulated with animal-like ease.

No, his appearance, his magnetism with women, was not in any doubt, and in other circumstances Darrell might have felt wary of him. But to counteract this feeling, there was the presence of Celine Lawford, his wife.

She was the discordant note in the whole proceedings, and Darrell had been unable to avoid noticing how unsuited she was to her present surroundings. Small and slender, with a cap of silvery blonde hair framing her piquantly attractive face, Celine was as striking as her husband, but it was obvious that she neither liked nor made any effort to mix with Matthew's family. It was evident in the bored expression she had worn throughout the ceremony, and afterwards at the reception she had made it painfully apparent that she considered the arrangements gauche and lacking in refinement. Clearly, she had not attended the wedding willingly, and she considered her husband's relatives coarse and vulgar.

It wasn't true, of course. The Lawfords were a friendly crowd, and during the eight months Darrell had lived in Sedgeley, she had grown very fond of these down-to-earth northern people. But she, like everyone else, had had to learn to accept them for what they were and not try to change them. They had no time for artifice or pretension, whereas Celine no doubt was used to the bland sophistication of city life.

Matthew Lawford was different. Darrell had had to admit that to herself. He had fitted back into his surroundings with the ease of a chameleon, swallowing beers in the pub before the wedding with his father and four younger brothers as if he was used to doing this every day of his life. The Lawfords were a large family, Susan had two older married sisters as well as the younger one who had been bridesmaid, but it was Matthew who appeared to be the family favourite, and to be charitable Darrell had at first thought that Celine was jealous. She might well be, but it wasn't just that. Whatever feelings she had for her husband, she cared nothing for his family, and Darrell had hoped that her attitude wouldn't spoil Susan's day. It hadn't. The Lawford clan was too closeknit for that.

"Having problems?"

The attractive unfamiliar voice brought Darrell's head up with a jerk to find the subject of her thoughts standing right in front of her, regarding her steadily. "Oh – not really," she demurred, with a rueful smile. "It's my fault for coming out here."

Matthew's eyes travelled down to the toes of her shoes emerging from the hem of her gown. "It was pretty humid in there, though, wasn't it?" he commented, looking into her eyes again. He had a disturbingly direct stare that disconcerted her. "You're Miss Anderson, aren't you? Susan's nursing friend?"

"Darrell Anderson," supplied Darrell, nodding. "It's a pity it's been such a miserable day."

"Do you believe in omens, Miss Anderson?" he enquired, and she thought he was teasing her.

"Not really."

"Nor do I." He smiled. "Would you believe I got married in a heatwave?"

Darrell found herself smiling, but she couldn't help it, even though his remark had been outrageous. "I – are you going back to London tonight, Mr. Lawford?"

"You know who I am, then?"

Darrell looked up at him in surprise, and in spite of her five feet six inches she had to look *up* at him, holding her

8

boater on to the back of her head. "Of course. You're Susan's brother."

"And do you call all her brothers *Mr*. Lawford?"

Darrell shook her head, and he nodded. "So – the name's Matthew, or Matt, if you'd rather. That's what the family call me. And no, I'm not driving back to London tonight."

Darrell could feel her hair working loose from the coronet she had secured on top of her head, and red-gold tendrils were tumbling about her ears. Dropping the hem of her skirt, she gave herself up to securing her hair, taking off her hat and sighing resignedly.

"I think I'm fighting a losing battle, don't you?" she asked lightly, and then pointed into the marquee behind them. "Oh, look! Susan and Frank are leaving."

The bride and groom left in a shower of confetti, the crowd surging after them to wave them off, and Darrell felt Matthew's hand close round her wrist for a moment to prevent her from being swept along with them. For a moment she was close against him, his chest hard against the softness of her full breasts. Then he had set her free again and was saying apologetically: "Sorry about that, but people get carried away here – literally!" He smiled. "I understand my mother has invited you to join us at the house this evening. They don't allow the excuse for a freak-out to go unchallenged around here. Perhaps you've noticed. Not that they'd call it a freak-out," he amended wryly. "A knees-up, perhaps." He paused. "Anyway, if you'd like to go home and change first, my car's at your disposal."

Darrell didn't know what to say. She, who was usually so cool and collected with men, felt as nervous as a schoolgirl on her first date, and the feeling was unfamiliar and not altogether pleasant. She didn't even know why she was feeling this way. Matthew Lawford had been amusing and polite, but nothing

9

more. He was no doubt used to making small talk with his wife's friends, and it meant no more to him than that. But a few moments ago, when his fingers had fastened round her wrist, she had experienced a terrifying new sensation that bore little resemblance to casual acquaintanceship.

"I – er – I came with Doctor Morrison and his wife – from the hospital," she explained awkwardly. "I expect I'll go home with them. I can always get a bus back later." She glanced at her watch as though to confirm this. "After all, it's only half past four."

Matthew Lawford inclined his head. "If that's what you prefer."

Darrell felt terrible. It wasn't what she preferred at all, but something, some inner sense warned her that further association with this man would be dangerous for her. She glanced round and saw to her relief that people were coming back again. The bride and groom had left for the bride's home in Windsor Street to get changed. Pretty soon, the reception would break up and only the family and close friends would gather later on at the house. She felt vaguely relieved when another of Susan's brothers came to join them.

Jeff Lawford was twenty-two, a year younger than Darrell, and a welder at a local steel works. For the past three months, he had been trying to persuade Darrell to go out with him, and he smiled at her now, flicking a speculative glance towards his older brother.

"Well?" he commented. "It went off very well, didn't it? In spite of the lousy weather!"

"Susan looked beautiful," exclaimed Darrell enthusiastically and Jeff gave her an old-fashioned look.

"Susan could never look beautiful!" he asserted with brotherly candour. "But she did look nice." He surveyed Darrell thoroughly and with evident approval. "Now, if you had been the bride . . ."

Darrell coloured. "Oh, Jeff!"

"What's wrong? With that red hair, you'd be a sensation!"

"It's not red," she retorted. "It's darker than that."

"If you say so." Jeff grinned, and then slapped Matthew on the shoulder. "Fancy a beer, Matt?"

Matthew flexed his shoulder muscles. "I wouldn't say no," he conceded, glancing at Darrell. "Will you excuse us?"

"Of course."

Darrell managed a smile in return, and then breathed a sigh almost of relief as they moved away. A small, motherly little woman was approaching her, and she turned to greet Susan's mother with real warmth.

"Oh, Darrell," said Mrs. Lawford, patting her arm. "I haven't had a minute to talk to you since this morning. How did it go? Did you enjoy yourself? Did everyone have enough to eat and drink, do you think?"

Darrell relaxed. "Oh, of course they did. The meal was delicious. And everything went off perfectly. Susan looked a dream, didn't she?"

"Do you think so?" Mrs. Lawford beamed with motherly pride. "I must say, I thought she looked really lovely. She and Frank have gone back to the house to change. I'm hoping they'll be able to slip away unobserved. You know how it is."

"That's what I'm planning to do, too," remarked Darrell dryly, indicating the hat in her hand. "My hair's coming loose, and this dress is beginning to annoy me."

"Oh, but you looked lovely, dear. You have such pretty colouring. And your hair always looks nicer, loose about your shoulders." She gave an encompassing look around her. "You are coming over this evening, aren't you? I'm expecting you to. The boys will be there, and Evelyn and Jennifer and their husbands. Matt's staying over, too. Have you met Matt yet?"

"Oh – y-yes." Darrell's fingers tortured the brim of the boater. "I was talking to him a few moments ago."

"Were you, dear?" Mrs. Lawford wasn't really listening to her. She clicked her tongue impatiently. "Oh – there's Celine sitting over there looking as if butter wouldn't melt in her mouth! Why doesn't she try to join in the fun? She's done her best to spoil the day!"

"I expect she feels out of place," murmured Darrell, unconsciously allaying a little of the guilt she felt about her attraction to Matthew, by defending his wife. "She doesn't come from Sedgeley, does she?"

"Heavens, no." Mrs. Lawford made a gesture of negation. "She was Celine Galbraith before she married Matt. Her father's an important man in the city, and the family own some estate in Wiltshire. Thinks herself too good for the likes of us, she does."

"Oh, Mrs. Lawford . . ."

"Don't you think so?"

Darrell shrugged awkwardly. "It's not for me to say."

Mrs. Lawford's sniff was expressive. "Well, how about you coming over and having a word with her? Perhaps she'll take to you – you being from the south, like."

Darrell wanted to demur, but Mrs. Lawford was already moving away and she had, perforce, to follow her. Celine looked up languidly at their approach, her expression mirroring her boredom at the proceedings.

"There now, Celine," exclaimed Mrs. Lawford comfortably. "I've brought someone to see you. This is Darrell Anderson, Susan's friend from the hospital. They're nurses together."

"Isn't that nice?" Celine drawled sardonically, looking up at Darrell without enthusiasm. Close to, Darrell could see the fine lines of dissipation about Celine's eyes, and a certain nervous agitation in the way they darted about. "We were

12

introduced earlier, weren't we?"

Darrell nodded. "Yes. At the house. Before the wedding."

"Ah, yes." Celine's lips curled as her mother-in-law moved away. "You don't come from around here, do you?"

"No, I'm afraid not. I was born in Essex. In Upminster, actually. Do you know it?"

"Do I not! Civilised country!" Celine uttered a short laugh. "Don't be afraid to tell anyone, my dear. Who'd want to come from around here anyway?"

"I like it," defended Darrell at once. "I love the north. It's so much – cleaner, for one thing."

"Cleaner! Sedgeley?" Celine shook her head pityingly. "You can't be serious!"

"I am. You don't get the diesel fumes up here that you get in and around London. Besides, there's more room to breathe – to live!"

Celine's mouth twisted cynically. "I can see they've got to you all right."

"No one's *got* to me. I mean it. I really like it here."

"Well, sit down," Celine invited, patting the wooden seat beside hers. "At least we can talk about somewhere else, even if you don't find Sedgeley a pain in the neck."

"I'm afraid I can't do that." Darrell had no desire to prolong this *tête-à-tête*. "I'm leaving now. I want to go home and change. Mrs. Lawford has invited me over to the house this evening."

"Oh, *lord*!" Celine uttered a groan of dismay. "The family get-together! Oh, God, why can't Matthew take me back to London tonight?"

There was no answer Darrell could make to this and with a faint smile she began to move away. But Celine got to her feet and halted her with: "Where do you live?"

Darrell hesitated. "Susan and I used to share a flat near

the hospital. I'm keeping it on until I can find someone else to share."

"The hospital?" Celine frowned. "Is that near here?"

"No. It's on the outskirts of Sedgeley. At the other side of town."

"Is it?" Celine sounded interested. "And do you have your own transport?'

"Well – no," Darrell answered reluctantly. "I – I came with one of the doctors and his wife."

"Very well." Celine brightened. "I'll take you home."

"Oh, no." Darrell flushed uncomfortably. She had somehow known this was coming. "That is – it's not necessary, Mrs. Lawford."

"Damn it, I know it's not." Celine made an irritated gesture. "I just need an excuse to get away from Matthew's family for a while, that's all. You can make me a decent cup of coffee, and then I can bring you back again. How's that?"

Darrell sighed, looking round helplessly. What could she say? That she had already refused Celine's husband's offer to take her home? That she had no desire to spend time with the wife of a man who she felt could quite easily disrupt the peace and tranquillity of her hitherto organised existence?

To her intense relief she saw Matthew Lawford coming towards them, accompanied by his elder sister, Evelyn. Darrell had learned that although Matthew was the eldest of the five sons, he had two older sisters. He moved with indolent grace through the thronging groups of friends and relatives, exchanging a word here and there, laughing at some remark passed to him, and making some equally amusing comment in return, judging from the loud guffaws that followed him. Darrell guessed they were the usual lewd jokes made at weddings everywhere, but Celine was looking distinctly out of humour.

Reaching his wife and Darrell, Matthew glanced at each of them in turn, his brows lifted interrogatively. "Have you two been getting to know one another?"

"We're just leaving, actually," returned Celine, before Darrell could say anything. "I've offered to run Susan's friend home. You have no objections to me taking the car, do you?"

Matthew's eyes probed Darrell's, and she could feel herself going hot all over. "I – I've just been explaining to your wife that Doctor Morrison is taking me home," she defended herself, and Evelyn smiled.

"There's no need for you to bother, Celine," she put in calmly. "Jeff's been wanting the chance to get Darrell to himself for the past six months. I'm sure he'd jump at the chance of taking her home."

"But – " began Darrell, only to be silenced by Celine stalking off and leaving them all wrapped in a moment's pregnant silence.

Matthew seemed the least affected by the embarrassment that followed. "Well," he mused, "you appear to have lost that opportunity," and Evelyn's lips twitched uncontrollably.

"Oh, Matt!" she exclaimed. Then she looked at Darrell. "Come along, Darrell. If the worst comes to the worst, I can always take you home."

Darrell was beginning to feel like an unnecessary encumbrance, but she went with Evelyn, mainly because she wanted to avoid being alone with Matthew Lawford. She was sure his eyes followed their progress across the marquee and consequently she stumbled and would have fallen had not a hand reached out and saved her. She looked up gratefully into Elizabeth Morrison's smiling face.

"So there you are, Darrell," the doctor's wife exclaimed. "Adrian's looking for you. We're leaving now."

Evelyn halted and turned. "You are, Mrs. Morrison?" She

looked at Darrell. "Well, isn't that a coincidence?"

Darrell nodded with relief. A coincidence indeed!

The flat was cool, and felt abnormally empty, which was ridiculous because it at least had not changed. Two bedrooms, living room, kitchen and bathroom, it sounded spacious; but as the two girls had learned the two bedrooms were in effect one large bedroom converted into two, the kitchen was an alcove off the living area, and the bathroom was scarcely big enough to turn round in. Still, in spite of the indifferent furnishings provided by the owners, it was home, but without Susan's irritating clutter it was empty.

Darrell stripped off the long coffee-coloured gown, and examined the hem, determinedly keeping her thoughts on the mundane matters. Apart from several mud stains which would possibly brush off when they were completely dry, it was in reasonable order and she was relieved. Her mother had bought her the dress for her last birthday, and she would have hated to have faced her wrath if the dress had been permanently marked.

Pulling on a housecoat, she went into the tiny kitchen and switched on the kettle. A cup of tea was what she needed after all that wine. A cup of tea and several quiet minutes to compose herself for the evening's festivities ahead of her. Perhaps she could ring and excuse herself, she thought doubtfully. She could always invent a headache. But the recollection of Celine's attitude towards the Lawford family made her think again.

Mrs. Lawford would be terribly disappointed if she failed to put in an appearance. Perhaps she would imagine that she, Darrell, felt out of place in such partisan society. Which wouldn't be true. Darrell had always enjoyed her visit to the Lawford house. They had always made her feel so welcome, encompassing her in the kind of family atmosphere she had never experienced with her own parents.

The kettle boiled and she made the tea, carrying the tray through to the living room and setting it down on a low table beside the couch. As she poured the tea, she reflected that it was hardly surprising that she had never known what it was like to be part of a family. Her parents had divorced when she was seven years old, which at the time had come as a blessed relief after years of listening to her parents quarrelling. Her father had been to blame, or that was her mother's story and the fact that her father had married again within a year of obtaining the decree had seemed to bear out that theory. Darrell had been too young to judge at that time, and it was only as she had grown older she had begun to appreciate that there were always two sides to every situation. Her father's second wife was young, younger than her mother had been, and within a few years they had produced two sons who might well have been brothers to Darrell, if her mother had let them. But throughout her childhood, she had jealously guarded her daughter, allowing her to visit her father only rarely, and consequently, by the time Darrell was old enough to judge for herself, her half-brothers had formed their own opinions of her. Delia, her stepmother, had hardened, too, and Darrell did not really feel at home with them. She knew her father regretted this bitterly, but he was naturally more inclined to be loyal to the family he had made.

Darrell's mother, who had been a designer working for a firm of textile manufacturers at the time of her marriage, had picked up the pieces after the break rather well. She had opened her own interior decorating business, and was now much sought after by her wealthy London clients. Even before her move to Sedgeley, Darrell had grown accustomed to seeing little of her mother, and her own work at the hospital,

17

living in the nurses' hostel there, had created a gulf which neither of them particularly wished to bridge now.

That was why Darrell had found the Lawfords' ebullience and generosity so warming and appealing. She had responded to the teasing and bantering and good-natured arguing that went on within the family circle, and she had often wished that she could have had that kind of background instead of being a part of two beings who had each in their own way chosen to live their own lives of which she had no part.

She sighed. Weddings were always a time for sentimentality. She was allowing the emptiness of the flat to get through to her. It was foolish. Sooner or later she would have to find someone else to share the place with her, and that was a prospect she did not relish. She and Susan had got along so well together, and the fact that Susan had been instrumental in finding the flat and suggesting they shared it, had made it more of a mutual arrangement somehow.

Finishing her tea, she got to her feet and walked to the window. It had begun to rain in earnest again, and the sky hung grey and overcast over the houses opposite. Lucky Susan and Frank, off to Majorca. At least it wouldn't be raining there.

With a grimace, she collected the tray and carried it back into the kitchen. She made herself a sandwich in lieu of an evening meal, and then went to change. She decided to wear a cotton corduroy slack suit and a plain brown shirt. The suit was cream and toned well with her matt complexion. She considered calling a taxi to take her across town because the bus stop was several yards away from the street in which the flat was situated, but it seemed an extravagance, so instead she donned her navy poplin coat and picked up her umbrella.

She ran to the end of the road and fortunately caught a bus almost immediately. Jolting along through Sedgeley town centre, she reflected wryly that had she accepted Celine Lawford's offer of a lift she would have avoided all this. But at what cost? What on earth would they have talked about?

The bus deposited her in the market place, and from there she had to catch another bus out to Windsor Street. This time she was not so lucky and spent fifteen minutes standing in the bus shelter waiting for the connection.

It was after eight by the time she was walking up Windsor Street to the Lawfords' house, but she could hear the sounds of merriment before she reached their door. The record player was going full blast, and there was the sound of raised voices and laughter. For a moment she hung back, half deterred at the thought of so many strangers. Although she knew Susan's immediate family, she did not know all the aunts and uncles, cousins and in-laws that constituted the whole Lawford clan, and she was an outsider, after all.

But then the door opened and Penny Lawford was standing smiling at her, her brother Jeff jostling for a position behind her.

"Come on in, Darrell," she exclaimed, stepping back on to Jeff's foot and grimacing at his agonised protest. "We were beginning to wonder whether you were going to make it. Take your coat off. You're soaked!"

Within minutes, Darrell was engulfed into the family circle, a glass of something strong and warming was pressed into her hand and she was thrust into the lounge which seemed to be overflowing with people.

Jeff limped after her, rubbing his ankle. "I'm glad you came, Darrell," he said, and she knew he meant it.

"Did Susan and Frank get away without too much fuss?" she asked, trying not to be aware that there was no sign of either Matthew Lawford or his wife.

"Well, Matt's taken them to Leeds," Jeff explained, pulling the tab off a can of beer and raising it to his lips. "Mike and I managed to fill Frank's pyjama legs full of confetti, but that was last night. I don't think he would open the case to check on them this morning. He had quite a hangover after last night's little celebration." He grinned reminiscently.

"Oh, Jeff!" Darrell could well imagine Susan's consternation if Frank pulled out his pyjamas and emptied their contents all over their bedroom floor in the hotel at Porto Cristo. "What a rotten thing to do!"

Jeff chuckled. "It's expected. And our Susan was too fly to leave her cases lying around. She locked them up last night, do you know that? Slept with the key of the cupboard under her pillow!"

"Good for Susan!" Darrell sipped her drink and then gasped as the fiery spirit burned the back of her throat. "What is this?"

Jeff put his head on one side. "Well, it's supposed to be punch – Dad's style. I believe it's a mixture of whisky, rum, brandy and vodka."

"I don't believe you."

Jeff shrugged. "Please yourself. Knowing Dad, that's likely to be a conservative estimate."

Darrell smiled in answer to a greeting called to her across the room from Mrs. Lawford and took another sip of the fiery mixture. "Ugh!" She shivered. "I can't drink this. It's – horrible!"

Jeff raised his eyebrows mockingly. "Don't let Dad hear you say that."

"Why not? I've noticed that all he drinks is beer – like you."

"Punch isn't a man's tipple."

"And beer is, I suppose?"

Jeff nodded, finishing the can in his hand. "Come on, let's dance."

The Lawfords' home was a rambling old terrace house which Mr. Lawford and his sons had converted by knocking down walls and putting in central heating. Consequently, the lounge now stretched from the front to the back of the property and was big enough to accommodate the rapidly expanding needs of the family. Tonight, a space had been cleared at the end for dancing, and several couples were already abandoning themselves to the beat music when Darrell allowed Jeff to propel her to join them. She had been glad to dispose of her drink on to a side table and determined not to be duped into drinking any more punch.

It was hot, and after a few minutes Darrell had to stop to take off her jacket and unfasten the top couple of buttons of her blouse. She had left her hair loose this evening, but now she wished she had at least brought an elastic band to lift it off her neck.

"Where's Celine?" she managed to ask Jeff in one of the intervals between records, and he shrugged, glancing round indifferently.

"I don't know," he replied. "She wanted to go with Matt and the others, but there wasn't room in the car and she wasn't suited."

"There wasn't room in the car . . .?" Darrell looked confused. "Why? What sort of car was it?"

"Oh, it's a big B.M.W.," remarked Jeff enviously. "But all the kids wanted to go. You know. Evelyn's two and our Jennifer's Christine. They wanted to go out to the airport, so Matt said they could."

"I see," Darrell nodded.

"Anyway, they should have been back by now. They'd have been here already, but the flight was delayed an hour.

One of those last-minute hitches. Hey – I made a pun! Did you notice that? A hitch for the hitched!"

He laughed and Penny and her boy-friend and one or two of the others who had been dancing came to see what was so funny. There was a lot of goodnatured chaffing going on and Darrell turned away, raising her arms to tug her fingers through her tangled hair. The effort tautened the material of her shirt across her breasts, although she was unaware of it, but as she stood there straightening her arms into a stretch she became aware of the group of young people just entering the lounge, and over their heads her eyes encountered the dark eyes of Matthew Lawford. There was a disturbing moment when he held her gaze, and then she turned abruptly away, catching Jeff's arm and saying: "I thought you asked me to dance!"

CHAPTER TWO

The alarm rang insistently, and Darrell groaned and rolled over to switch it off. Seven o'clock! Who would choose to get up at such an unearthly hour? she thought impatiently, sliding out of bed before succumbing once more to the waves of drowsiness that were tugging at her consciousness. She spared a thought for Susan as she dressed, waking on the morning after her wedding night. Darrell decided wryly that whatever she might be doing at this moment, it would not entail swallowing a hasty breakfast and reporting for ward duty at eight a.m.

The hospital was only a ten-minute walk away from the flat, and this morning the sun was forcing its way through the low-hanging clouds as Darrell set off. Now that she was fully awake, she was glad she was going to work. The brisk routine of the hospital would give her little time to dwell on the disturbing aspects of the previous day's events.

Not that anything particularly momentous had happened,

she acknowledged. Her feelings were the result of an over-active imagination and Matthew Lawford had treated her no differently from any one of the other girls present at the reception. But for her there had been something – something in the way he looked at her, in the way he spoke to her, which, whether he intended it or not, and she was sure he didn't, had disrupted her emotions to a disquieting extent.

She had told herself it was the wine, that she was un-accustomed to alcohol, but in fact she had not drunk a lot. Nevertheless, it had been a shattering experience to realise that in spite of always believing herself capable of controlling any situation, he had disconcerted her without any apparent effort on his part. It was galling. She felt like a schoolgirl with her first crush, and she despised herself for it. The more so because Matthew Lawford was not only way out of her sphere, but married as well. He might be Susan's brother, he might be able to submerge his personality into his brothers' mould when it suited him to do so – but basically he was different, and that, no doubt, was why Celine had married him.

Celine!

Darrell could not suppress a shiver when she recalled the scene which had taken place the night before after Matthew's return from Leeds.

Until then, Celine had not been in evidence, but it had turned out later that she had been lying down upstairs, ostensibly nursing a headache. As soon as her husband returned, however, she came downstairs, still wearing the turquoise crêpe dress she had worn for the wedding, which now looked rather creased.

Darrell had been dancing with Mike Lawford, another of the brothers. Without admitting it to herself, she had been staying with the younger members of the family deliberately, avoiding any possible contact with Matthew. But she had been unable to avoid overhearing the words that had passed between them. Celine had been determined that everyone should hear.

She had begun by complaining that she couldn't possibly stay in the house a moment longer, her head was throbbing, she said, and the music was driving her mad. To be charitable, Darrell had had to concede that if Celine did indeed have a headache, she might well have been feeling desperate, but it soon became apparent that this was not the only reason why she wanted to leave. As her voice became shriller and her words more slurred, Darrell realised that Celine was more than a little intoxicated.

Matthew had endeavoured to persuade her, mildly at first, that he couldn't leave yet, that he had only just arrived, and that his parents expected him to stay. His mother, joining them, had even suggested that perhaps Celine might like to go home with Evelyn when she took the younger children to bed, and stay the night there where it would be peaceful.

But Celine wanted none of this. The prospect of spending the night with any of Matthew's relatives was clearly not a good idea so far as she was concerned, and she demanded that Matthew go and book her a suite of rooms in the best hotel in town.

And this was when the argument had become less tolerant. Matthew had stated flatly that he had no intention of booking rooms in any hotel when his own family were perfectly prepared to accommodate them, and when Celine started to criticise his family he told her bluntly that he would not bring the Lawford name into disrepute in the town by revealing his wife's imperfections.

It had become a terrible slanging match, with Matthew controlling his temper admirably. Inevitably, Celine had burst into tears and Mrs. Lawford, with her innate kindness, had led her daughter-in-law away and calmed her with coffee and aspirins.

But Celine's behaviour had put a damper on the party, and when Jeff suggested that he and Darrell and some of the others went on to the nightclub in the town, they had all been eager to agree. Consequently, Darrell had arrived home in the early hours of the morning feeling exhausted and distinctly depressed.

Sunday was not usually a busy day at the Sedgeley General and the morning dragged by until lunchtime when there was an emergency appendectomy in the theatre. Darrell had her lunch with Carol Withers, a fellow staff nurse, in the hospital canteen, and then returned to the surgical ward until the evening. Visitors were allowed for two hours during the afternoon, and as there were no further emergencies, Darrell was able to write up her reports in Sister's office without interruption. There was a minor upheaval soon after tea when the patient who had had the appendectomy recovered consciousness and was sick all over his bed, but the sheets were soon changed and Darrell spent several minutes assuring the poor man that he had not been the nuisance he imagined. Then it was time to hand over to the night staff, and Darrell collected her cape and handbag and left the building.

It had been an unsettled day, periodically raining and then becoming sunny, but the evening was quite delightful, the sky almost completely rid of the clouds which had caused the showers. She walked down Hollyhurst Road feeling more relaxed than she had done walking up it that morning, and was shocked out of her reverie when a long gunmetal grey car pulled alongside her. She didn't recognise the car. It belonged to no one she knew, she was sure – an impression which was quickly allayed when Matthew Lawford climbed out.

He was wearing a dark suit in some sort of soft suede, and his tie was very black against his white shirt. The thick brown hair lay smoothly against his head, and his thick lashes hid the expression in his eyes. There were lines beside his mouth which she didn't think had been there yesterday, and a feathering of anticipation slid along her spine.

"Hello, Darrell," he greeted her quietly. "I've been waiting for you."

"For me?" Darrell glanced all round her, as though she couldn't believe he was addressing her, but the road was almost deserted. Then she looked into the car, and it was empty, too. Hot colour ran up her cheeks. "I – I don't understand." Or did she? "Why are you waiting for me?"

Matthew swung open the passenger side door. "Get inside," he directed. "I have to talk to you."

Darrell didn't know what to say. All her emotions clamoured for her to do as he asked, but cold logic kept her standing on the pavement. "Whatever it is – whatever it is you have to say to me, can't – can't it be said here?" she stammered.

His eyes were narrowed. "What's the matter, Darrell? Don't you trust me?" he enquired, his voice acquiring an edge of coldness.

Darrell felt terrible. "It's not that. Oh – oh, very well."

With many misgivings, she climbed into the front of the car and he slammed her door before walking round to slide in beside her. He closed his door, but he did not immediately start the engine, and she tensed.

"It's about Susan – Susan and Frank," he told her steadily. "I gather you haven't heard the news today?"

"The news? What news?"

Darrell was hopelessly confused, but something in his tone stirred a ripple of cold premonition inside her.

Matthew sighed. "There's been a crash, Darrell," he replied

tonelessly. "Late last night. But it was early this morning before we got the news . . ."

"News?" Darrell stared at him blankly. Then: "You can't mean – you don't mean – the plane – "

Matthew looked down at his hand resting lightly on the wheel. "Susan and Frank are dead, Darrell – "

"Oh, no!"

"– they were killed instantly, I think. There were no survivors."

"Oh, no!" Darrell moved her head disbelievingly from side to side. "It can't be true. It mustn't be true!"

"But it is true, Darrell. I assure you." Matthew drew a steadying breath. "How do you think the family feel? How do you think my mother feels? My father . . ." He shook his head. "Well, he's getting good and drunk, but my mother . . ." He paused. "Will you come?"

Darrell nodded, pressing trembling hands to her cheeks, feeling the prick of tears behind her lids. Matthew looked at her, as though to assure himself that she was all right, and that direct stare was the undoing of her. Unable to prevent herself, she burst into tears, feeling the salty drops wetting her hands as they streamed unheeded down her cheeks. It had all been too much – the tension over the wedding and Celine's outburst, her own troubled feelings towards Matthew, and now this . . . Poor Susan! Poor Frank! Not even their wedding night had been spared them . . .

With an exclamation, Matthew reached for her, pulling her against him, putting his arms around her and pressing her face against his chest. He had unbuttoned his jacket and his shirt was smooth and silky against her cheek. Beneath its softness she could feel the hardness of muscle, smell the shaving lotion he wore, inhale the clean fragrance of his skin. His heart was beating steadily in her ears, and his strength was something she badly needed just at this moment. But alongside this feeling were other feelings, and it was the knowledge of their presence even in these moments of stress which forced her to draw back from him and search blindly for a tissue.

"I'm sorry," she said. "I'm not normally so emotional. It was just a such a – such a terrible – shock!"

"I know," Matthew nodded, buttoning his jacket again as he turned to the wheel. His voice was strangely taut as he commented: "It's better to cry if you can. Releases tension, isn't that what they say?"

Darrell dried her eyes. "I suppose so. Could we – that is – I'd rather not go – like this." She indicated her uniform selfconsciously.

Matthew started the engine and swung the powerful car away from the kerb. "Just direct me to where you live," he answered. "I'll wait while you change."

When they reached the flats, Darrell turned to him. "I – will you come in?" she invited awkwardly.

"Would you rather I didn't?"

Darrell hesitated a moment and then shook her head. "No, please – come in."

Matthew made a gesture of acquiescence and as she fumbled her way out of the door at her side, he climbed out easily and locked the car.

The cream emulsioned walls of the apartment building had never seemed more drab, the stair treads bare and worn in the centre. Darrell led the way upstairs on unsteady legs, finding her key and inserting it in the lock.

Matthew stood in the centre of the living room looking about him with what she felt sure must be feigned interest. He had never been here while Susan was living in the flat, and now that she was dead . . . *Dead*! She still couldn't believe it.

"I won't be a minute," she said, flinging her handbag on to

a chair and indicating the couch. "Won't you sit down? I'm afraid I don't have anything alcoholic I can offer you, but there's coffee . . ."

"Thank you." Matthew was polite. "But I don't want anything. Take your time. There's no hurry."

Darrell left him sitting on the couch and entered her bedroom. As she took off her uniform she surreptitiously examined her face in the dressing table mirror. She looked pale, much paler than usual, and there were blotches round her eyes where she had been crying. What a mess! What must he think of her? She sighed, shaking her head impatiently. Don't do getting the wrong ideas about this, she told herself severely. It had been kind of him to come and break the news, but that was all.

She dressed in a plain navy skirt and a cream blouse, brushing her hair out of the severe chignon she wore for working, and securing it behind her ears with two combs. Cold water had removed almost all traces of grief, and a careful use of a moisturising foundation cream erased the rest. She didn't bother with any other make-up, she seldom wore a lot anyway, and the result was still very pale, but composed.

Matthew rose to his feet as she re-entered the lounge, a dark blue suede coat over her arm. His eyes flickered over her briefly, and then he said: "You're ready?"

Darrell nodded.

"Have you eaten?"

Darrell frowned. "Why – no. But it doesn't matter. I'm not feeling much like eating anyway."

Matthew thrust his hands into his jacket pockets. "You must eat something. As a nurse you should know that."

Darrell glanced round helplessly. "It's all right – really."

Matthew regarded her for another unblinking moment, then he shrugged. "Come along, then."

It was amazing how quickly one could reach Windsor Street if one did not have to rely on buses, Darrell thought bleakly, trying to put the picture of Susan and Frank's mangled bodies out of her mind. One could by-pass the town centre completely, taking the direct route on the ring road. There were plenty of cars about on this warm summer evening and it seemed incredible that for most of these people another plane crash would arouse nothing more than an exclamation of sympathy for those involved. But for Susan and Frank . . .

She pressed her lips tightly together. She must not get emotional, not now. She had been Susan's friend, but the Lawfords were her family, her flesh and blood. Somehow she had to be strong enough to bear their grief and absorb some of it if she could.

Matthew, who had been silent on the journey, glanced sideways at her as they turned into Windsor Street. "This is going to be pretty harrowing for you, Darrell," he said quietly. "But thank you for coming. My mother – all of us – appreciate it."

His words affected her more than her thoughts had done, and she nodded quickly, not trusting herself to speak. When the powerful car drew to a halt at the Lawfords' gate, she thrust open her door and climbed out before she succumbed to the crazy desire to comfort him as he had comforted her a little while ago.

The next few hours were gruelling ones as Matthew had predicted. The house seemed full of people, and the kettle was constantly boiling to make tea. Relatives from out of town who had attended the wedding the day before and who had been staying overnight before returning home were still there, and there was a lack of organisation that Mrs. Lawford would never have permitted had she not been stricken with her own grief. She gathered herself sufficiently to tell Darrell that the airline was sending all the bodies home for burial, and that Evelyn and her husband had flown out to Palma, at the airline's expense, to attend to the details on their behalf. Frank's father had gone too, she said, but Mr. Lawford was in no fit state to go anywhere. Darrell guessed what it must have cost her to tell an outsider this, and respected her for it.

Darrell herself was soon busy in the kitchen, washing dishes and generally making use of herself. There was still a certain amount of disorder left from the night before, and she stacked cakes and pastries into tins and threw out dozens of empty bottles and sandwiches whose edges had curled unappetisingly. Penny, the Lawfords' youngest daughter, appeared from time to time, her eyes red-rimmed from crying. She was no assistance, but Jennifer, the other married sister, remained by her mother's side. Darrell understood that at a time like this Mrs. Lawford needed someone to lean on.

Susan's brothers seemed to have taken over the dining room and were keeping out of the way. The majority of people milling around were aunts and uncles and cousins, and one or two of Frank's relatives. Laura Vincent, Mrs. Lawford's sister, came to help Darrell with the washing up and it was she who explained how the news had been broken in the early hours of the morning.

"We hadn't heard any news, you see," she said, shaking her head. "Not having the television on, or anything. Frank's family were getting ready to go home when these policemen came to the door."

"It must have been terrible," put in Darrell sympathetically, and Laura nodded.

"It was – *terrible*! Our Margaret just collapsed, and Jim – well, he – he wouldn't believe it."

"I still find it hard to believe," murmured Darrell, with feeling.

Laura picked up a cup and began polishing it absently with the teacloth. "It was just as well our Matt was here. He was a tower of strength. Pulled his mother round, he did. I don't know what she'd have done if that toffee-nosed wife of his had had her way and they'd left directly after the wedding. That was what she wanted to do, you know. And causing that scene after tea! Conceited, that's what she is. Thinks herself too good for the likes of us!"

"Oh, please . . ." Darrell didn't want to get involved in a discussion about Celine Lawford. "Er – Evelyn left this morning, then?"

"For Palma, yes. Matt would have gone himself, but our Margaret begged him to stay. The funeral's likely to be on Thursday. Joint affair, so I believe. Susan and Frank. *Susan and Frank!*"

Tears appeared at the corners of her eyes and she dabbed them away. But it was difficult to remain immune from the awful tragedy of it all.

Darrell was making fresh sandwiches in an effort to tempt the men to eat something at least when the kitchen door opened and Celine came in. Up until then, Darrell had assumed she must have got her way and been installed in some hotel, but it was obvious from the petulance of her expression that this was not so.

Heaving a heavy sigh, she came and perched on the corner of the table, watching Darrell working with a jaundiced eye. "You must like being here," she commented, grimacing. "Imagine coming back at a time like this."

There was no evidence of grief in Celine's bored expression and Darrell wondered that anyone could remain unmoved by what had occurred. Particularly when that someone was so close to the family. But then Celine would probably tell her that she was not close to the family. She probably hadn't met Susan above a dozen times. They were virtually strangers to her. All the same, even a stranger might find it difficult not to respond to the pathos of it all.

"I hope someone's hungry." Darrell avoided any open confrontation. "I wonder if everyone likes cheese with chutney."

"I suppose, being a nurse, you're used to situations like this," remarked Celine, bringing a pack of cigarettes out of the pocket of her well cut slacks. Although she was small, she was very slender, and the masculine attire accentuated her femininity.

Darrell nodded now. This at least was safer ground. "Yes. Although one never quite learns to accept it."

Celine lit her cigarette. "Oh, come on," she exclaimed. "You don't mean to tell me you feel for every passing corpse that comes your way!"

Darrell didn't care for her turn of phrase. "Death is always unexpected," she replied carefully. "I can never quite get over the feeling of loss when two people are in a room together and suddenly one of them –" She broke off. "I'm sorry. That was morbid of me." She quartered the pile of sandwiches and began arranging them on a plate. "When – when are you leaving? After – the funeral?"

Celine exhaled smoke through her nostrils, looking irritable. "God alone knows, I don't! Matthew should have left today at the latest. He has a board meeting tomorrow afternoon, and he leaves for New York on Wednesday."

Darrell turned to rinse her fingers at the sink. "I – I believe the funeral's not until Thursday," she murmured.

"I know that. But Matthew's a busy man, his work is important. He can't just neglect everything because there's been a plane crash . . ."

"It is a family bereavement," Darrell pointed out quietly.

"Do you think I'm not aware of that, too? My God, it's been thrust down my throat ever since I came here. Family this – family that. It's sickening! What has Matthew in common with his family now? He doesn't live like they do, he doesn't think like they do, he doesn't act like they do. His world is not their world. All right, so Susan's dead, and that's a pity. But you could count on one hand the number of times he's seen her in the last five years!"

"Nevertheless, she was his sister, and his mother needs his support –"

"His mother needs his support! What about me? Don't I need his support, too? My God, what has his mother ever done for him? What has his blessed family ever done for him?"

Darrell dried her hands and found a tray for the sandwiches. "If you'll excuse me . . ." she murmured uncomfortably.

Celine slid off the table and paced restlessly about the kitchen. "Oh, yes, go on, go and play nursemaid to all of them. I'm superfluous here. I'm not even allowed a lousy drink to drown my sorrows, do you know that?" She snorted angrily. "Tea – that's all they can think about. The universal panacea. Well, not for me!"

Darrell determinedly excused herself and left the kitchen. She knocked at the dining room door and went in. The younger Lawford brothers were playing cards at the table, while Matthew and the next oldest brother Martin were standing together, talking in low tones. Martin was married, too, but his wife, Alison, came from Sedgeley, and as she was eight months pregnant at this time was spending the day with her own parents. They all looked up at Darrell's entrance, and Jeff made an effort to act naturally.

"That was a kind idea, Darrell," he said, getting up and

taking the tray from her. "What have we here? Cheese? Ham?"

"It's a mixture. Some are cheese and chutney, some are ham. It was all I could find, I'm afraid."

"Well, I'm starving," announced David Lawford, getting up as well and taking one of the sandwiches. He was eighteen and the youngest of the brothers. "Is there any beer? I could do with a drink as well."

"I know where there's some lager," said Jeff, putting the tray on the table.

"I'll make tea, if you'd rather," ventured Darrell, but David shook his head.

"I think we've had enough tea today," he replied, with a faint smile. "What about you? Are you going to join us?"

"Oh, no." Darrell backed towards the door, conscious of Matthew's eyes upon her. "No, I've got plenty to do. I'll tell your mother you're having something to eat in here."

"When you want to leave, let me know." Matthew spoke for the first time, and Darrell could feel the colour running up her cheeks.

"I can take Darrell home," interjected Jeff, looking impatiently at his brother.

"I brought her here, so naturally I'll take her home," retorted Matthew coolly, and Jeff reached for a sandwich with ill grace.

"I suppose your car is more comfortable than my mini," he muttered, with his mouth full, and Darrell shifted uncomfortably.

"I can always take the bus – or get a taxi," she murmured. "Er – if you'll excuse me . . ."

To her relief, Celine had gone when she got back to the kitchen, but Mrs. Lawford was there.

"Oh, there you are, Darrell," she exclaimed. "I was looking

for you. Dr. Morrison's here, and I think he'd like to see you."

"Dr. Morrison? Would like to see me?" Darrell was confused.

"Yes. He – he came to offer his condolences." Mrs. Lawford sniffed, and then controlled herself. "Come along, child. Don't keep him waiting."

Adrian Morrison was standing in the hall, talking to Mrs. Lawford's sister, but he looked up with some relief himself when Darrell appeared. Mrs. Lawford beckoned her sister away, and the doctor turned to her understandingly.

"We've just had the news," he said, "and I wanted you to know that if you'd like a few days off, I'm sure it can be arranged."

"But Doctor Morrison –"

"Look, Darrell, this must have been a terrible shock to you. You may not wholly realise yet exactly how shocked you are. You know as well as I do the effects of delayed reaction. And Mrs. Lawford tells me you're being a great help to her –"

"I'm only washing a few dishes –"

"Nevertheless, someone has to do it, and she's glad of your company."

"What? With all these people . . ."

"Sometimes friends are of more comfort than relatives, Darrell. You know that. Besides, you and Susan were very close. It's natural that her mother should see you as a kind of link . . ." He paused. "Anyway, I'm told that the funeral is to be on Thursday. I suggest you take the next week off, and come back to work a week tomorrow. I'll speak to Matron."

"But I couldn't!"

"Why not?"

"Well, with Susan – I mean – you're short-staffed, as it is."

"We'll manage. We're not such a small establishment that we can't compensate for one indispensable staff nurse!"

Darrell wrapped her arms closely about herself. "I didn't mean that."

"I know. But don't worry, we can cope. And if we should run into difficulties, I can always send out an S.O.S., can't I?"

Darrell managed a smile. "Thank you."

After he had gone, Mrs. Lawford came to find her. "Well?" she urged. "What did he say?"

Darrell sighed. "He's given me the week off."

"Oh, I am glad." Mrs. Lawford squeezed her shoulder warmly. "I told him you and Susan had been like sisters to one another. He was very understanding."

Darrell opened her mouth to protest, and then closed it again. She and Susan had been close. Perhaps not as close as sisters, but then sisters were not always close to one another. And they had shared the flat for the past eight months. She would have missed her anyway, but this . . .

"You'll stay here, of course," went on Mrs. Lawford, but at this Darrell shook her head.

"No. No, I'll stay at the flat. I'd rather. Besides, it's no use me getting used to having a lot of company. It would make it all the worse when – when I had to go back."

Mrs. Lawford studied her pale face for several seconds, and then she nodded. "All right, Darrell, I can appreciate that. Now – how about a nice cup of tea?"

Evelyn telephoned from Palma soon after ten, and Mr. Lawford roused himself to come downstairs and listen to the call. Formalities there were taking longer than expected, and Evelyn did not expect to return home until Tuesday at the earliest. Fortunately, the bodies were recognisable, the plane having ploughed into a hillside and killed most people on impact. This made things easier for the authorities, and less harrowing for the relatives, but it was still a gruelling experience and Evelyn could not hide her emotion when she heard her father's voice. There seemed little doubt, she said, that the crash had been the result of an error on the part of the pilot, coming in too low over the mountains and then failing to gain altitude again when it became apparent that he was descending too fast. There were a number of theories, of course, but this seemed to be the most consistent one.

By the time the call was over, they were all feeling the strain of a renewed awareness of the tragedy that had occurred. For a while its sharpness had been blunted, but now it was as acute as ever. It would take many more than twenty-four hours for them all to accept the finality of it all.

It was after eleven when Darrell washed up the last few dishes, and went to find her jacket. It was hung over the banister in the hall and she was putting it on when Matthew came out of the lounge.

"Are you ready to leave?" he enquired politely.

Darrell heaved a sigh. "Yes. But you don't have to take me. I mean – I can easily call a cab."

"Why? My car's outside. I said I would take you home."

"I know you did." Darrell's fingers tightened round her handbag. "But—"

"Would you rather Jeff took you home?" he asked, that direct stare devastating her.

"I don't want to trouble anybody."

"It's no trouble. I'm quite prepared to take you."

Mrs. Lawford appeared behind her son. "Leaving now, Darrell, are you? That's right. You go and get a good night's sleep. We'll see you tomorrow. And thank you for all you've done."

Darrell moved awkwardly. "I've done nothing," she protested.

Mrs. Lawford managed a smile. "Don't you believe it." She turned to her eldest son. "You're taking Darrell home, aren't you, Matt? Drive carefully, won't you? We don't want . . ." She allowed the remainder of the sentence to go unsaid, but her meaning was obvious.

Matthew's eyes challenged Darrell to contradict his mother, and with a sigh she went to the door of the lounge and called goodnight to the others. Celine was there, sitting moodily on the arm of a chair, staring at the television which was playing away entirely for her benefit. Everyone else was talking. Darrell half hoped she would look up and offer to go with them, but apart from an irritated glance in Darrell's direction, she made no move. The inevitable cigarette was dangling from her fingers, and she smoked it with swift nervous gestures.

Outside the big B.M.W. looked incongruous in the narrow street. Jeff's Mini was parked behind it, and Matthew viewed his brother's vehicle with vague impatience.

"I can get Jeff's keys if you've rather go in the Mini," he suggested dryly, and Darrell stood by the door of the B.M.W., waiting for him to open it, feeling decidedly put out.

The drive across town was accomplished as silently as they had come, and it seemed no time at all before they were drawing up outside the apartment building. Only then did Darrell feel a sense of contrition at her childish behaviour

"Thank you," she said, glancing at him reluctantly.

"No sweat." He shrugged indifferently. Then, as she was about to get out, he added quietly: "You must tell me if I'm interrupting some scene you and Jeff have got going for you. I got the impression, perhaps mistakenly, from Susan, that you were not interested."

"I'm not – that is –" Darrell broke off awkwardly. "I'm sorry if I was – ungrateful. I'm not, truly. It's just – well, I'm tired, I suppose, and not very tactful."

He half turned in his seat towards her, his face shadowed in the light from the street lamps. "Why should you need to be tactful?" he asked softly. "That's a curious expression to use."

Darrell sighed. "It was a figure of speech, that's all. I – oh, goodnight, Mr. Lawford. And thank you again."

With trembling fingers, she thrust open the door and climbed out, slamming it behind her. Then she ran up the steps into the building, stopping with a thumping heart when she heard footsteps behind her.

"Come on," he said, taking her arm, "I'll see you into the flat. I don't like the idea of you coming home alone at this time of night."

Darrell had no choice but to agree, although his fingers at her elbow sent little electric currents down her veins into her hand. He released her at her door and she sought the key in the bottom of her bag, inserting it in the lock with unsteady fingers. Once the door was open and the lamps switched on, she turned back to him with feigned nonchalance.

"You see – no intruders!" she remarked lightly.

"Why are you afraid of me, Darrell?" he asked unexpectedly, one hand supporting himself against the open door.

"Af-afraid of you?" Darrell faltered. "I don't know what you mean."

Matthew studied her suddenly heated cheeks with resignation. "Yes, you do," he returned flatly. "You're as nervous as a wild cat when I'm around. Why? What do you expect me to do to you? What has Susan told you about me that's given me such a bad reputation?"

Darrell gasped. "I – you're imagining things, Mr. Lawford."

"Am I?" Matthew folded his arms. "I wonder." He smiled,

41

but it was a rather twisted sort of smile. "Did she tell you that I live some kind of amoral life? That I mix with people whose whole object in life is the pursuit of pleasure? Well, maybe she was right. The codes I live by might not go down too well in a place like Sedgeley. But I am not without conscience, *Miss* Anderson, and contrary to belief, I've never been unfaithful to my wife!"

Darrell didn't know where to look or what to say. She felt totally and completely demoralised, the more so because she had judged him without scruples.

"So . . ." Matthew turned to go out the door, "I'll say goodnight. My mother told me you've been given the week off, so no doubt we'll see one another again. Goodbye."

The door closed behind him and Darrell stood staring at it feeling sick and distraught. And this time, it had nothing to do with Susan and Frank.

CHAPTER THREE

Although she was physically exhausted, Darrell found it impossible to sleep. Eventually, in the early hours of the morning, she got up and took several aspirins, and she must have fallen into a drugged slumber because when she opened her eyes again it was after ten o'clock.

Her head ached as she made herself some coffee and forced a slice of toast down her throat. Depression was gripping her, and she delayed going round to the Lawfords' until the last possible moment. She chided herself for being a coward, for selfishly thinking of her own feelings at a time like this, and then when she got there she found that Matthew and his wife had left for London that morning and were not expected back until Wednesday afternoon. This should have aroused some relief, but curiously enough it didn't.

The house seemed strangely quiet. Mr. Lawford was still in bed, and the three sons still living at home had gone out. Jennifer, Penny and their mother were in the kitchen, and were obviously glad of an excuse to make another cup of tea.

Inevitably, the conversation came round to Matthew, and Penny said resentfully: "I never thought he'd go. I never thought he'd let her persuade him!"

"Now, Penny," said her mother, with a calming gesture, "Matt can't just stay at home from his job like you can. People depend on him for their livelihood. Why, Celine said he was supposed to be going to America on Wednesday!"

"All he's interested in is making money, money and more money," muttered Jenny, hunching her shoulders. "And what's it all for, that's what I'd like to know. You won't benefit from it."

Mrs. Lawford sighed. "Penny, you know your dad and I don't want Matt's money. We're quite happy as we are. We've got everything we need. This house has been good enough for us this far, and no doubt it'll still be here after we've gone."

"Well, I think you deserve a better house," retorted Jenny moodily. "He can afford it."

"Penny, Matt's paid for Patrick to go through university, and he's going to do the same for David if he gets the results. And he bought us that beautiful colour television –"

"A colour television!" grumbled Penny. "What's a colour telly? I bet they have one in every room, including the loo!"

"Oh, shut up, Penny," exclaimed Jennifer, looking apologetically at Darrell. "Darrell doesn't want to hear you moaning on. There are more important things to think about."

"That's right, Penny, there are," put in her mother, nodding. "Matt's done plenty for you. It's not his fault that you chose to leave school at sixteen and get a job in Prestwicks."

Penny sniffed. "I wanted to earn some money."

"There you are, then. You could have had a good education just like Patrick, but not you!"

Darrell endeavoured to change the conversation. "How is Mr. Lawford this morning?" she asked tentatively.

"I think he's going to be all right, Darrell," replied Mrs. Lawford, patting her hand. "He's coming round. Well, you have to, don't you? I mean life has to go on. We're lucky really. We still have three daughters. Frank was the Barclays' only son."

Darrell found the next three days dragged. In one way she knew she would have been better off at work, absorbing herself in the bustling activity of the hospital. But in another she realised that she herself was far from completely fit. Perhaps she had caught a cold on the day of the wedding, that damp rainy afternoon which had portended the gloom which was to come; and perhaps the shock had affected her more than she had thought. But whatever it was, the headache she had woken with on Monday morning had persisted, and by Wednesday afternoon she was feeling hot and feverish. It was only a head cold, but she thought she would feel better at home and told Mrs. Lawford so.

"All right, dear, you go," agreed the older woman, after expressing concern at her flushed appearance. "There's nothing much to be done here, and I expect Matt and Celine will be arriving shortly – "

"If he doesn't go to America," put in Penny bitterly, and her mother gave her an impatient look.

"Our Jeff can take you home," she went on, as though Penny hadn't spoken. "He's just sitting in the front room watching telly."

"Oh, no, really, I can get a bus," protested Darrell urgently. "Honestly, I'd prefer the exercise, and it's a lovely afternoon."

This at least was true. It was a beautiful afternoon, the sun was very hot and the sky was an arc of blue overhead. But

45

Darrell would have wanted to leave whatever the weather, she accepted that. The last thing she needed right now was a confrontation with Matthew and Celine.

Mrs. Lawford looked doubtful. "Well, I don't know . . ." she was beginning slowly, when the front door was opened and there were sounds of activity and voices from the hall. Darrell could hear Jeff's voice, and his father's, and another voice, an attractive male voice which was unmistakable.

"It's Matt!" exclaimed Penny, springing to her feet, her resentment vanishing in the face of her brother's return. "Hey, Matt!"

She rushed out of the kitchen and Mrs. Lawford looked apologetically at Darrell. "Well," she murmured, "at least Penny's fears were groundless. I knew he wouldn't go to America, I just knew it."

For the moment, Darrell's proposed departure was forgotten as Mrs. Lawford joined the other members of her family to greet her oldest son, and Darrell stood uncertainly in the kitchen wishing she could just leave the back way. But that would be cowardly, and besides, sooner or later, she had to meet him again.

So summoning all her courage she walked into the hall, staying in the background while the others exchanged greetings. There was no sign of Celine at the moment, but Matthew's dark eyes registered her appearance and he inclined his head politely in her direction.

Eventually Mrs. Lawford turned and saw her. "Are you going now, Darrell?" she asked gently. "We'll see you tomorrow, right?"

Darrell nodded, reaching for the white cardigan which was lying on the chest in the hall where she had dropped it on her arrival that morning. "Yes. I'll be around about eleven." She knew something would be expected of her and her eyes flickered swiftly over Matthew. "Hello – and goodbye, Mr. Lawford. I hope you had a good journey."

Matthew was in his shirt sleeves, a beige-coloured denim shirt that was opened down his chest and cream denim levis. He looked tired, as if the journey had wearied him, and there were deep engraved lines beside his eyes and mouth.

"Where are you going?" he asked, ignoring her greeting, and Mrs. Lawford said: "She's going home. She's full of cold. She must have caught a chill on – on Saturday."

"I'll take you," he said, flinging the jacket which was looped over one shoulder on to the chest. "What's five miles more or less after over two hundred?"

Penny's lips drooped. "But you've only just got here, Matt," she exclaimed petulantly.

"Don't be selfish, Penny," retorted Mrs. Lawford. "You know I wasn't happy about Darrell going home on the bus."

"I'd have taken her," said Jeff, and Darrell wanted to put her hands over her ears and scream at them that she was perfectly capable of making her own way home.

But Matthew's expression brooked no refusals today, and unwilling to enter into any more argument, she gave in, nodding her thanks and saying a terse goodbye to the rest of the family.

She half expected Celine to be waiting in the car, but it was empty, and her startled expression must have conveyed her thoughts to Matthew.

"She hasn't come," he stated flatly, swinging open the door for her to get inside. "Just hang on a minute!"

He went back up the path to the house and came back a few minutes later swinging the denim jacket that matched his trousers. He slung it into the back of the car and then got in beside her. She found herself surreptitiously watching him as he levered himself more comfortably behind the wheel,

47

noticing the gold watch on its leather strap round his wrist, the signet ring on the third finger of his left hand. The sign of a married man, she thought tensely. The smell of the heat of his body came to her in the limited confines of the car, and she thought how far he had already travelled that day. She ought to appreciate this.

The powerful car swung away from the kerb and cruised down the length of Windsor Street before emerging on to the main thoroughfare that joined the ring road. But instead of turning right towards Sedgeley, the car swung into the stream of cars going west towards the moors. Darrell's head jerked round in astonishment, and he said quietly: "I'm not about to kidnap you, but I could surely use a drink. Will you join me?"

"Do I have any choice?"

His lips thinned. "Yes. There's a turn-off along here that takes us back on to the ring road. Should I take it?"

Darrell hesitated a moment, and then she shook her head. "I'll have a drink with you. Thank you."

She shook back her hair, feeling the moist dampness on her forehead, and he glanced quickly at her. "I forgot. My mother said you were unwell. Would you rather go straight home?"

"No. No." Darrell shook her head again. "It's just a cold. I'll be all right."

Matthew gave her a brief assessing look, and then shrugged his broad shoulders. "You're the nurse," he commented dryly.

He took her to a small inn overlooking Scarsbeck reservoir. On this hot summer's afternoon, several sailing dinghies were dotted about its cool reaches, and as the inn was practically deserted, Matthew carried their drinks to a low stone wall overlooking the gravelled foreshore. He had got her something long and cool, heavily iced and edged with orange and lemon slices. He was drinking lager.

"Well?" he said, after she had swallowed a mouthful of her drink and gasped at its sharpness. "How is it?"

Darrell blinked. "Very refreshing."

He smiled. "Actually, I meant – how are things?"

"Oh." Darrell moved her shoulders helplessly. "Everything is being organised. They – that is – Susan and Frank's bodies arrived back yesterday afternoon, and were taken to the chapel as you had arranged. Jeff saw to that. And your father has taken over the rest of the arrangements."

Matthew nodded. "That's good. I thought he'd pull himself round. He's better when I'm away, I think."

"Was that why you went away?"

Matthew's lips twisted. "Oh, I could say that, couldn't I? Make out it was an unselfish gesture!" He shook his head, swallowing some of his lager. "Do you think anyone would believe it? Oh, no. I left for purely selfish reasons."

Darrell didn't know how to answer this, so she said nothing, and presently he went on: "However, I was supposed to leave for New York this morning, but in spite of much opposition, that I refused to do."

Darrell wondered if Celine had provided most of the opposition. "Do – do you visit the United States often?" she ventured.

Matthew stared broodingly down at the coloured sails below them. "I go where my work takes me," he said slowly. Then he looked up. "Do you know anything about applied economics?"

Darrell shook her head. "Not a lot, no. My father is a lecturer in history, and my mother is an interior decorator. Interior designing, she calls it."

"Where? Here in Sedgeley?" Matthew frowned.

"Heavens, no. She lives in Upminster, but her base is in London."

"What's the name of her company? Perhaps I know it."

"Allan Inter-Designs. My parents are divorced, and my mother uses her maiden name."

Matthew looked thoughtful. "It doesn't ring any bells, but Celine might know it. Her friends go in a lot for that sort of thing."

"Yes." Darrell felt uncomfortable at the mention of his wife's name. "And – and economics. That's your field, is it?"

Matthew finished his lager before nodding. "Business finance is a form of applied economics. It includes accounting, statistics, optimizing a firm's assets to their best advantage. It means arranging short-term credit loans and selling securities to raise long-term funds. Basically, we're juggling with figures, borrowing from one company to finance another."

Darrell was fascinated. "It sounds exciting."

"It can be." He rose to his feet. "Do you want another?" He indicated the still three-quarters-full glass in her hand.

"Oh, no." Darrell spread her fingers over the rim. "But you go ahead."

She watched him walk away across the gravelled forecourt. Although he had gone back for his jacket, he had not put it on, and his shirt was sticking to his back in places. She liked the way he moved, he had long legs, but they were strong and muscular, firm beneath the close-fitting cloth of his trousers.

She looked away impatiently. Oh, God, what was she thinking? Matthew Lawford was a married man. His wife was a young and beautiful woman, far more soignée and elegant than she would ever be. Any attention he might be showing her was simply an effort to alleviate his boredom during this time of family crisis.

She didn't watch him come back, but she heard his suede-booted feet crunching over the gravel, and a few moments later he came down beside her on the wall carrying a second glass of lager.

"Tell me," he said, after watching her averted face for several minutes, "what brought you to Sedgeley? You have no relatives here, do you?"

"No." Darrell sipped her drink. "Actually, I just felt like a change of scene."

"I know the feeling. But why Sedgeley?"

Darrell shrugged. "One of the girls at the hospital I used to work in in London came from here. She said, you want to try Sedgeley General. So I did."

"Was that how you got to know Susan?"

"That, and an introduction from Phyllis."

"Phyllis Collins?" Matthew looked amused.

"Why, yes. Do you know her?" Unaccountably her heart sank.

"Oh, yes, I know – or should I say, I *knew* Phyllis. Sedgeley girls who leave to go and work in London are not that thick on the ground. Besides, as you probably guessed, Phyl was a friend of Susan's."

"I see." Darrell looked down into her glass.

"Are you never homesick, or didn't you live at home?"

"I lived at the hospital in London, but I spent my free weekends with my mother. At least, some of them," she amended.

"What about your father? Did you see much of him?"

"Not a lot, no. He and Delia have their own family and friends."

"Delia?"

"My father married again. He and his wife had two sons."

Matthew nodded slowly. "Tough."

Darrell shifted defensively. She didn't want his pity. "It isn't really," she argued shortly. "I've never been used to having brothers and sisters around."

"Okay, okay," he said mildly. "I didn't know I was treading on any toes. I can be a tactless brute, I know that."

"You're not treading on any toes," retorted Darrell crossly. "My parents weren't happy together. It was a relief for all of us when they split up."

He allowed her words to go uncommented upon, staring out lazily across the water. She sighed, feeling strangely tearful. Somewhere someone was playing a guitar, and the melancholy sounds it emitted drifted on the still air.

After several minutes had elapsed, she said awkwardly: "We – won't your mother be wondering where you are? I mean, it only takes fifteen minutes to run me home."

Matthew turned to look at her, one thumb hooked in the low belt of his trousers. "You want to go?"

Darrell sighed again, impatiently now. "It's nothing to do with me. I just thought – oh, it doesn't matter."

Matthew finished the lager in his glass in a gulp and looked down into its emptiness. "All right," he said. "Let's go."

Darrell finished the liquid in her glass, handing it to him when he reached for it. He walked back into the inn to return the glasses and she stood up, dusting down her skirt. The cotton gingham dress was limp in the heat, moulding the rounded curves of her breasts, and its length left most of her legs bare. Smoothing her damp palms over her hips, she walked back to where Matthew had parked the car and was examining her profile in the wing mirror when he appeared.

He opened her door and she got in selfconsciously, tucking her skirt around her knees. Then he walked round the bonnet and got in beside her. Before starting the engine, he flexed his shoulder muscles and stifled a yawn.

"God, I'm tired," he grunted, half to himself, and she glanced uncertainly at him.

"You don't have to take me all the way home," she ventured, and then shrank away from the anger in his face.

"If you say that once more – " he muttered threateningly, and without another word started the motor.

They were soon back in Sedgeley, speeding along the wide circular route which led to Bardon Road. Matthew was an expert driver, the wheel slid effortlessly through his fingers, and his braking was all done smoothly with the gears. Darrell thought how pleasant it would be to drive a long distance with him, but knew she was hardly likely to experience such a thing.

He stopped at the entrance to the flats and she gave him a nervous smile. "Thank you. Thank you for the drink. I – I enjoyed it."

"My pleasure."

His voice was expressionless, and she had no idea what he was really thinking.

"I – I'll see you tomorrow, then," she murmured, opening the door.

"At the funeral, yes." He nodded, his face grim. "I shall be leaving for London straight after."

"Oh!" She couldn't control the sudden feeling of desolation which swept over her at this news. "Will you?" She paused. "Then I may not see you to speak to again."

"Alone? No." He was abrupt.

"Well – goodbye, then."

"Goodbye." He stared straight ahead through the windscreen, apparently more interested in the antics of a couple of children down the street than in her. He glanced her way as she closed the door, her fingers gripping the open window frame. "Remember me to Phyllis next time you see her," he said, and drove away.

Darrell's cold was a little improved in the morning. But her depression had increased, and she half wished her cold had been worse, bad enough to excuse herself from going to the funeral.

Then she got angry with herself for thinking so selfishly. This was her last opportunity to share anything with Susan, and she should not be thinking of her own problems at a time like this.

Nevertheless, it was difficult to dissociate one from the other. Without the event of the tragedy, Matthew would have gone back to London on the day after the wedding, and she might never have seen him again. As it was, she had seen far too much of him for her own peace of mind. But even that was foolishness. Never at any time had he treated her with anything more than friendly detachment. Except that evening in the flat when he had verbally censured her assessment of him . . .

Knowing there was no escape from this final confrontation slowed her step and she was only half dressed when the doorbell rang. Immediately, her heart sprang into her throat and she went to the door and called nervously: "Who is it?"

"Me! Jeff!"

"Oh!" Her pulses resumed their normal speed and she partially opened the door, sheltering behind it. "Is anything wrong?"

"No." Jeff looked very smart in his dark suit, his lean face pale and sombre. "Mum sent me to get you."

Darrell sighed, glancing down at her housecoat and then, deciding it was suitably modest, stepped away from the door.

"Come in, Jeff. I'm afraid I'm not ready, as you can see."

Jeff entered the flat and closed the door, leaning back against it. "That's okay, I can wait. I think Mum was worried in case you were any worse. How do you feel?"

Darrell turned away, running a careless hand over her silky curtain of hair. "Oh, I'm all right. Much better, as a matter of fact." She glanced back at him. "And, as it happens, I ordered a cab about half an hour ago. I didn't expect anyone to come for me."

"Not even Matt?" asked Jeff shortly, and then went bright red.

"What do you mean?" Darrell was taken aback.

"Oh, nothing." Jeff straightened, and looked uncomfortable.

"No." Darrell would not be put off. "You must have meant something."

Jeff sighed heavily. "Oh, I'm just fed up, I guess," he muttered. "Take no notice of me."

But Darrell couldn't do that. "Jeff, if there's something on your mind . . ."

"There's not." Jeff raked an impatient hand through his hair. "At least, not specially. Oh, I guess I'm just green with envy, Darrell, that's all. Matt has everything, hasn't he? I mean – that car, and a Jag. A super house in London, and a beautiful wife! What bloke wouldn't be jealous?"

"Oh! Oh, I see." Darrell felt the tautness go out of her. For a moment she had thought . . . She ran her tongue over dry lips. "Well, I'll go and finish getting ready, then." She walked to the bedroom door. "Cancel the cab for me, would you, Jeff? The number's on the pad."

She decided to wear the dark green suede suit her mother had bought her last Christmas. Whatever else her mother lacked, she had extremely good taste, and the plain skirt and close-fitting jacket drew attention to the firm lines of Darrell's figure. She hesitated longest over her hair, and then decided to leave it loose. Susan had liked it that way best.

Outside, another shock awaited her. The grey B.M.W. waited by the kerb, and for a few seconds she thought Matthew had come after all. But Jeff was unlocking the doors and swinging them open, grinning at her startled reaction.

"For your comfort, madam," he announced, forcing a brightness he was obviously far from feeling. "Seriously, though, you must admit it's an improvement."

Darrell drew an unsteady breath and got inside. The car was associated with too many memories she would rather forget. But no one else was aware of that but her.

The joint funeral processions were to leave from Windsor Street, and the Lawfords' house was full of people as it had been on the day of the wedding, but swelled by a number of neighbours and friends all wanting to offer their condolences. Darrell had little time during the next few hours to worry about her own affairs, and like everyone else she was affected by the poignancy of the occasion. The few times she caught a glimpse of Matthew, he was involved with other members of his family, and as Mrs. Lawford had almost collapsed just before they were due to leave for the church, he had plenty to do. There was no sign of Celine, however, and Darrell wondered how she could stay away at such a time.

After the service at the graveside, there was a reception at the Stag in Sedgeley, and Darrell found herself seated with Jennifer and her husband. Jennifer was managing to maintain a controlled façade now, and smiled at the girl who had been her sister's friend.

"I expect you're sick of the sight of us, aren't you, Darrell?" she exclaimed, with false brightness. "We all seem to have been in each other's pockets for the past week."

Darrell crumbled the roll on her plate. "I expect you'll be glad to get back to normal," she murmured.

Jennifer nodded. "Will I not!" She glanced at her husband. "Bill goes back to work tomorrow. He was going to wait until Monday, but the sooner we pick up the threads of our lives the better, don't you think?"

Darrell smiled her agreement. "Your mother is looking better."

Jennifer glanced along the table. "Yes, she is, isn't she? She's been marvellous – coping with everything when Dad took to his bed."

"Your father thought the world of Susan, and you know it," put in Bill quietly, and Jennifer looked down at her plate, schooling her features.

"I think what really broke Mum up was Celine not coming to the funeral," she went on bluntly. She looked at Darrell. "You noticed that our dear sister-in-law hasn't put in an appearance, didn't you, Darrell?"

"*Jennifer!*"

Bill's tone was reproving, but his wife ignored him. "Well! I'm sure that's what it was. We should have guessed something like this would happen when Matt took her back to London."

"Leave it, Jennifer."

"No, I won't. Matt could have *made* her come back with him."

"Perhaps he wasn't that bothered whether she came or not," retorted Bill sharply. "My God, who wants her at the funeral if she's only here under duress?"

"I still say it was a dirty trick."

Darrell shifted uncomfortably. She seemed fated to be the unwilling recipient of the family's opinions about Matthew's wife. Even so, without any bias, she had to admit that Celine's behaviour left a lot to be desired.

Mrs. Lawford came to find her as the reception was breaking up. "You'll come back to the house, Darrell, won't you?" she invited gently.

Darrell hesitated. "I – no, I don't think so, Mrs. Lawford, if you don't mind."

"You're very welcome."

"I know that, but – " Darrell moved her shoulders awkwardly. "I think I'd rather go straight home. And please – " she hastened on, "I don't need a lift."

Mrs. Lawford smiled. She had aged considerably during the past few days, but at last the lines of strain were beginning to lift. "As you like, my dear. But don't – don't stop coming to the house just because Susan is dead, will you? I mean, we've come to regard you as – well, as one of the family, I suppose. You'll always be our link with Susan."

"Thank you."

The older woman turned away, obviously emotionally disturbed by any words about her daughter, and with controlled movements Darrell made her way to the door. She hadn't the stamina to say goodbye to everybody at this time, so she slipped away without anyone being aware of her going.

Outside, the late afternoon sunlight was very warm, and she took off her jacket and draped it over her arm. She had decided to walk back to the flat. She was in the centre of Sedgeley, and it wasn't all that far, and besides, the exercise would do her good.

She unbuttoned her cream blouse as low as she dared, and walked slowly across the market square and into Jesmond Avenue. As she walked she tried to concentrate on the hospital and thus clear her mind of all troubling thoughts. She wondered if she ought to go back to work tomorrow as Bill was doing. There was nothing to do at the flat, one person didn't make much mess, and it would be lonely there without any company.

Unwillingly, she found herself wondering what time Matthew intended leaving for London. Would Celine be waiting for him there, eager now to placate him for her absence from the funeral? Would he forgive her, because he loved her? Or would they have another row like the one they had had at his parents' home? If they did, did they make up afterwards? Was that what had happened on that other occasion, on the day of the wedding? After she and Jeff and the others had left for the nightclub, had Matthew taken his wife upstairs and made love to her? The idea was so distasteful to her that she caught her breath at the implications of her feelings.

It was after five o'clock when she reached the flat, and she let herself in dully, hearing the telephone ringing almost in the background of her mind. Then, realising it was her telephone that was ringing, she went to answer it.

It was her mother, and there was relief in speaking to someone who had no connection with the events of the past few days.

"Darrell? Darrell, is that you? Wherever have you been? I've been trying to reach you for days!"

Darrell dropped her jacket and bag on to the nearby chair and sank down on to its arm. "I'm sorry, Mummy. I've been – out a lot."

"You don't have to tell me that. Good heavens, I was getting quite worried about you. Where have you been? Surely you haven't been working evenings at the hospital?"

"No, Mummy. I – I've been at the Lawfords'."

"The Lawfords?" Her mother sounded vague. "Oh, yes, I remember. Isn't that the name of the girl you share the flat with?"

59

"It was, yes." Darrell paused. "You remember I told you, she was getting married last Saturday."

"Oh, yes, that's right. I do remember, now you mention it. Did everything go off all right?"

"The wedding was fine, but . . . but . . ."

"But what?" Her mother spoke sharply. "Don't tell me the marriage is on the rocks already!"

In other circumstances, Darrell could have laughed. Her mother always jumped to those sort of conclusions. It came from a certain cynicism towards men.

"You may have heard about a plane crash near Palma," she went on slowly. "Susan and Frank were on that plane."

There was silence for a moment and then her mother uttered a shocked exclamation. "You mean – they were *killed*?"

"Yes."

"Oh, Darrell! Oh, Darrell, what a terrible thing to happen!"

"It was rather." Darrell's throat felt tight.

"And – how have her family taken it?"

"How do you expect? It was a disaster. They – she and her husband – were buried today."

She could hear her mother making little shocked sounds. "And have you been at work?" Mrs. Anderson asked at last.

"Not since Sunday, no. Doctor Morrison gave me a week off."

"A week? Then you're not due back at the hospital until Monday?"

"Not officially, no."

"What does that mean?"

"Well, I was thinking of going back tomorrow."

"Why?"

Darrell sighed. "There's nothing else to do."

"Come home," said her mother at once. "Come here for the

60

weekend. You haven't been home for weeks. And you know you're always welcome."

Darrell hesitated. "I don't know, Mummy . . ."

"Why not? I wouldn't expect you to stay in all the time. You could go out – meet your friends. It would make a break for you."

Darrell thought hard. It would make a break, as her mother said, and she was not really keen to go back to work even though it would have solved the loneliness problem.

"Well," she began, "well, all right. I – I'll catch a train from Leeds in the morning. I don't know what time I'll get there. Expect me when you see me."

"Very well. You have your key, don't you, just in case I'm out."

Darrell nodded resignedly. "Yes, I have my key," she agreed, knowing full well that it was far more likely that she would be staying at home while her mother went out, rather than the other way around. Still, it would be something to take her mind off other things. Off Matthew . . .

She replaced the receiver carefully, and took a deep breath. If she was going away in the morning, she had packing to do and arrangements to make. Kicking off her wedge-heeled shoes, she picked up her jacket and was on her way to her bedroom when the doorbell rang.

Dropping the coat again, she padded on stockinged feet to the door, opening it cautiously. Then a surprised gasp escaped her. Matthew was standing just outside her door, his shirt collar unbuttoned and his tie hanging loosely below it.

"Hello, Darrell," he said, his tones flat and devoid of feeling. "Can I come in?"

Darrell stepped back without speaking, holding on to the door like a lifeline, and he came inside so that she could close it again. Pressing her palms back against the panels behind her, she said: "I – I thought you were leaving for – for London."

Matthew ran a hand round the back of his neck and walked into the middle of the room. "I was. I did." He shook his head. "As far as the family's concerned, I left for London fifteen minutes ago."

CHAPTER FOUR

"I see." Darrell was overwhelmingly conscious of her half open blouse and stockinged feet. "Was there – I mean, did you want something else?"

Matthew looked at her across the space between them, his eyes dark and disturbing. But for once he didn't hold her gaze. He looked away, saying: "Yes. Yes, I could use a drink. Do you have anything?"

Darrell swallowed with difficulty. "Nothing alcoholic, I'm afraid. Some – some Coke."

"Fine."

He walked across to the windows to stand with his back to her, and she hurried into the kitchen and took a can of Coke from the refrigerator. She refused to speculate on his reasons for coming here. For the moment, it was enough that he had come.

"Here you are." She came back into the living room and held out the can and a glass. He turned to take them, putting the glass on the window ledge and pulling the twist of metal enabling him to drink from the can.

While he drank, Darrell surreptitiously tidied the room, putting newspapers and magazines into the rack, shifting her shoes and shaking the cushions on the couch.

Then she straightened and began to button her blouse, but he came towards her and stopped her, one long finger stroking an imaginary line from just below her chin to the shadowy hollow between her breasts. His hands were very brown against her creamy flesh, and he bent his head and followed the line of his finger with his lips.

Darrell trembled violently and pulled herself away from him, breathing shallowly, gulping air into her tortured lungs. "Please – please, don't," she implored, turning her back on him. "I – I think you'd better go now."

Matthew tossed the empty Coke can into the waste bin and tugged his fingers down through his hair to the back of his neck. "Yes," he muttered, moving his head in a positive gesture. "I'm – sorry."

Darrell bent her head. "It's – it's all right," she managed, thinking hysterically that nothing could be further from the truth. "It – the funeral – it was a strain for everyone."

"Do you imagine I've come here for sympathy?" he demanded savagely, moving closer to her so that she could feel his breath fanning the nape of her neck. "Do you think that's all I want? Oh, *God*, if only it were!"

Darrell lifted her head. "What – what else could it be?"

"I thought you knew," he groaned, and then with an angry ejaculation he jerked her back against him, his hands sliding possessively over her breasts, holding her against him so that she could feel every straining muscle of his taut body. "Dear God, Darrell, don't you know I've wanted to do this since I saw you struggling in the mud last Saturday?"

"You can't – you don't know what you're saying—"

"I can and I do," he said unevenly, his mouth against her neck. "You were right to be wary of me, Darrell. I've proved myself every bit as amoral as you suspected."

Darrell, struggling to free herself, heard the curious catch in his voice, the thread of self-derision that conflicted with his self-denunciation, and twisted round in his arms to stare at him. His face was very pale, there was a hungry brilliance in his eyes, and a mocking humour tugged at the corners of his mouth.

"Well?" he challenged, his hands gripping her waist, allowing her to hold him at bay with her palms firm against his chest. "Haven't you anything to say to me? Like – I told you so? Like – I'm just another married man who wants to make love to a beautiful girl?"

"I – I don't believe that you are." Darrell was confused. "Why are you saying these things?"

"I suppose my next line should be that my wife doesn't understand me, that we're completely incompatible!" She didn't know whether he was taunting himself or her.

"Matt—" she began, but he stopped her.

"What? Isn't this what you expect to hear? Isn't this the usual explanation?"

"Stop it!" She drew her hands away from him, but the action only served to bring him closer. "You don't have to say anything. I – I don't want to know."

"Don't you?" He forced her face up to his. "But this has to be done right. You must forgive me if I'm a little out of practice with the current jargon—"

"Matt! Why are you doing this?" she cried. "Don't you want to touch me?"

Matthew expelled his breath harshly. "But I am touching you, aren't I, Darrell? This is your body mine is abusing, isn't it?" He bent his head, and his tongue trailed along her cheek. "And you know as well as I do that a man like me is not to be trusted."

Darrell's breathing was erratic. She didn't know what to think. "Do – do I know that?"

"You should." Matthew's voice hardened as he continued to cover her face with kisses. But he avoided touching her mouth, and she found herself aching for him to do so.

Then, as suddenly, he thrust her away from him, closing his eyes as though fighting for control. When he opened them again, their brilliance was muted by the thickness of his lashes. "So," he said through his teeth. "I'm no better than any other man." His smile was not pleasant. "How Celine would love to see me like this!"

Darrell's cheeks flamed. "I think you ought to go."

"So do I, oh, God! So do I!" he muttered violently. "But I don't want to. Do you know why I came here? I might as well be honest. I want you. I want to make love to you. And it's a long time since I've said that to any woman, including Celine!"

Darrell was trembling so much she doubted her legs would support her for much longer. "I don't want to hear about Celine," she whispered huskily, and he shook his head.

"I know. That would be unfair. Sufficient to say that – for the first time, I want to be unfaithful to my wife."

"Don't – don't you love her?"

"Don't I love Celine?" His expression was derisive. "Do you think I should?" He paused. Then: "No. No, I don't love her. I don't suppose I ever did. But then I wouldn't presume to imagine that Celine ever loved me. We – suited one another, at the time. It seemed a satisfactory arrangement."

"You're very cynical."

"But honest," he agreed wryly.

"Are you?" She was unknowingly provocative, standing there before him, her hair loose about her face, accentuating green eyes made luminous by her emotions. The blouse, taut across her breasts, drew his attention to their swelling fullness, as they rose and fell in her distress. "I think you want me to believe the worst about you. Why? Does that assuage your guilt?"

"My guilt? Oh, God!" he muttered grimly. "Nothing could assuage that!" He shook his head. "I never intended this to happen. I don't get involved with other women. My work means everything to me. Or at least, it has done up till now."

"And now?" Darrell couldn't resist the probe.

"Now – now—" He bent his head. "You know what's happened now as well as I do. It may be some time since I felt this fire in my loins, but I haven't forgotten what it means!"

"Oh, Matt!"

His words disarmed her, and she felt an overwhelming sense of longing to comfort him. But it was madness. It must be suppressed. How could she be sure he was telling the truth? It might just be a line to gain her sympathy. And yet something told her it was not, that Matthew despised himself for his weakness, that he did not entirely welcome this feeling he had for her. But what feeling was it? And what did he expect of her?

He was looking steadily at her. "You know what I'm asking, don't you?"

"I – don't – know . . ."

"I have no right, but – I want to stay—"

"Stay? You mean – all night?" Darrell wrapped her arms about her. The trembling had begun inside her, and she couldn't stop it.

"Yes."

"That's – impossible—"

"Why is it impossible?"

"Because . . ." Darrell shifted from one foot to the other. "Because – because it is."

"I need you, Darrell. And I believe you need me."

"I – need – you?" She was incredulous.

"That's what I said. You knew what was happening to us – that was why you tried to avoid me. Don't deny it. I knew it, too. But . . . God help me, I tried to put you out of my mind. It didn't work. I've thought of nothing else but you all through these terrible days!"

"Oh, *Matt!*"

His need was bearable, his grief was not. She couldn't hold out against him any longer. He was right – she did need him.

Without speaking, she nodded her head, and started when Matthew pulled off his tie and jacket and dropped them on to a chair. She had expected him to take her in his arms then, and when he didn't, she felt chilled.

"I could use a bath," he said, matter-of-factly. "Is that possible?"

Darrell gathered herself with difficulty. "Why – yes, of course."

"So where's the bathroom?"

Matthew was reassuringly gentle and she led the way through her bedroom into the kiosk that served as a bathroom. "There's plenty of soap and the towels are behind the door," she told him jerkily.

"Fine. I shan't be long." He looked down at her intently.

"Take as long as you like," she managed, and left him.

In the living room, she became aware of a dull throbbing behind her temples. It was nervous reaction, she knew it, but she couldn't help it. The full realisation of what she had committed herself to was sweeping over her and her mind recoiled from the recklessness of her decision.

Forcing a calmness she was far from feeling, she glanced at her watch. It was after six. No doubt her headache was due in part to hunger. Perhaps she should prepare a meal, something to sustain her through the ordeal.

The ordeal!

She felt vaguely hysterical. This was a situation she had never experienced. For a girl of her age she was unusually inexperienced. Her parents' broken marriage had always been there to warn her against the dangers of promiscuity. Her mother had already been pregnant at the time of their marriage, otherwise it was extremely doubtful that it would ever have taken place. Consequently, Darrell had never indulged in the free and easy involvements approved by other girls of her age, and although she understood the biology that drove a man and woman together, its more intimate aspects were unknown to her. Still, Matthew was not to know this, and she had no doubt that a woman's body held no secrets from him.

Going into the kitchen, she examined the contents of the refrigerator. As she had practically been living at the Lawfords' for the past week, there was little in there to inspire her. Some bacon, eggs, a few tomatoes, but that was all.

An examination of the food cupboard was almost as disappointing. Beans, peas, tinned fruit and vegetables, and a packet containing a Spanish omelette mix. Deciding omelettes were the most adequate nourishment she could think of, she whipped eggs in a basin and added the Spanish omelette mix. The result smelt very appetising, and she sliced tomatoes ready to fry with the omelettes.

When it was all prepared, she went back into the living room and paced about the floor. She had no idea how long Matthew would take, but she wanted to be making it by the time he reappeared. It would give her a few more minutes' grace.

She glanced down at the green suede skirt and cream blouse. Hardly the attire for an evening, she thought doubtfully. Perhaps if she put on a long skirt, or her turquoise silk caftan she would feel better. At least it would give her something to do. But she couldn't change in her bedroom where Matthew was likely to come upon her at any moment. She would collect the clothes and change in Su – in the *other* room. She winced. For a moment, the real reason for Matthew being in Sedgeley struck her, and tears burned at the backs of her eyes. Who was taking advantage of whom? she demanded achingly. Would Matthew ever have noticed her if Susan had not been killed?

She crossed the room and flung open her bedroom door, and then stopped aghast. Matthew had had his bath and was now stretched full length on her bed without a stitch of clothing. He was lying on his stomach, and it was only when she ventured: "*Matthew?*" tentatively that she realised he was asleep.

Her throat felt dry as she stood there just looking at him, and as she looked she realised that Matthew was not just any man in her life, but *the* man, the man she loved . . .

It was a terrifying apprehension, a bitter perception that drove all other thoughts from her mind. Matthew was not available. Whatever they shared was purely a temporary diversion. He was married . . . *married* . . .

She closed the door again and leant back against it sickly. Then she straightened and walked across the room. He was exhausted, and why not? Since driving up from London the previous day he had never stopped. So – she would not wake him. Not even if he slept all night . . .

The telephone shrilled around eight-thirty and she hastened to answer it. To her dismay, it was Jeff, wanting to know if she was all right.

"Yes. Yes, I'm fine," she got out jerkily.

"Would you like me to come round? I could – easily. I've had it with the family."

"Oh, no – please!" Darrell was overwhelmingly conscious of the fact that the B.M.W. must be parked outside. "That is – I'm just getting ready for bed, Jeff."

"At eight-thirty?" Jeff sounded sceptical.

"Yes. As – as a matter of fact, I'm going away tomorrow."

"Where are you going? London?"

"Yes."

"A pity you weren't leaving today, then."

"Wh – why?"

"Well, Matt left this afternoon. You could have driven down with him."

"Oh! Oh, I see."

Darrell glanced guiltily towards her bedroom door, wondering what Jeff's reaction would be if he knew that Matthew was not on his way to London at all, but here, in her flat. She could guess what he would think, and a wave of self-disgust swept over her.

"Well, I guess that's it, then," went on Jeff resignedly. "Sorry I troubled you."

Darrell couldn't let that go. "You didn't – trouble me, Jeff. I – I – thank you for ringing. It – it was thoughtful of you."

"But you don't want to know, I know."

"I didn't say that."

"You didn't have to. Okay, Darrell, I won't push my luck. Can I give you a ring after the weekend?"

"Of course. I'll be here."

"Fine. I'll be seeing you."

"Yes. G'bye, Jeff."

Darrell replaced the receiver quietly and then crossed to

71

her bedroom door and put her ear to the panels. There was no sound from within and on impulse she turned the handle and opened the door. Matthew was still lying on her bed, but now his eyes were wide open and staring at her.

"Oh!" Darrell was almost as shocked as when she had first found him on her bed. "You're awake," she murmured unnecessarily.

"What did he want?" Matthew asked sombrely.

"Wh – who?"

"Don't fool around, Darrell. I know it was Jeff."

"Oh! Oh, yes. On the telephone." Darrell hesitated. "He just wanted to see if I was all right."

"He wanted to come round, didn't he?"

"I – well, yes."

"Why didn't you say so?"

"Is this inquisition necessary?" Darrell glanced back into the living room. "I – er – I beat up some eggs earlier. Would you like an omelette?"

Matthew propped himself up on his elbows. "No, thanks." He paused significantly. "Come here."

Darrell swallowed convulsively. "Are you sure there's nothing you want? I mean – a drink? Some coffee? Or another Coke?"

"I said – come here," he repeated steadily.

"I – I –" Darrell wrung her hands together and turned away. "No. No, I can't."

Silence. For a minute, she thought he had accepted this, and then his hands descended on her shoulders and she was propelled back against him.

"What are you afraid of?" he probed, caressing the sides of her neck with his thumbs. "The situation may be new to me, but the needs of it aren't."

"I'm sure they're not," she answered weakly.

"So why are you playing hard to get?" he asked roughly, and twisting her round in his arms, he kissed her mouth with hard compelling urgency.

Her clothes were no barrier to the pressure of his body, and lethargy swept over her, parting her lips, moulding her body to his. No man had ever kissed her with such brutal intimacy, caressing her in such a way that the blood thundered through her ears and her senses swam. When her fingers encountered the pelt of fine dark hair that covered his chest down to his navel, he trembled violently, pressing her hands against him and devouring her with his mouth.

"Now, Darrell," he groaned against her lips. "Don't make me wait any longer."

But his words penetrated the fantasy world that was engulfing her, and to her dismay she felt a salty wetness stinging her cheeks. Matthew felt it too, and drew back abruptly to stare into her eyes, a scowl marring his lean features. He wiped a tear from her nose with a curious finger, and then said harshly: "Why in God's name are you crying?"

Darrell swallowed her breath as she started to reply and almost choked. "I – I don't know," she got out at last, when she was able to speak.

Matthew stared at her for a few seconds longer and then he pushed her away from him and walked across the room to where he had left his clothes. Darrell stood watching him miserably as he pulled on his trousers and then turned to regard her grimly.

"Why did you do it, Darrell?" he demanded bitterly. "If it was just a game you were playing, it's a dangerous pastime. I doubt whether anyone else but me would be fool enough to let you get away with it."

Darrell pressed her lips tightly together. "Matt, you – you don't understand—"

"You're damn right, I don't." He reached for his shirt and slid his arms into the sleeves. "You're a continual box of surprises, do you know that? All right, I shouldn't have come here – I accept that. But I made my feelings clear. You knew . . ." He broke off. "I just don't understand why you've changed your mind. Is it because I'm married?" He was contemptuous. "I can't believe that could make such a difference."

"Matt, listen to me!" she implored.

"Why? So you can tell me some imaginary tale about being scared and never having done this sort of thing before?"

"*I haven't !*" she burst out tremulously, and was devastated by the scepticism in his gaze.

"Oh, no? But I suppose you're madly in love with me and that's why you decided to give way this time."

Darrell's lips parted. "Yes," she admitted desperately, "yes, that's exactly how it happened."

"God Almighty!" Briefly Matthew raised his eyes heavenward, and then stared at her as if she was mad. "What lengths women will go to – what lies they'll tell to get their own way!"

"It – it's the truth!" she whispered brokenly, already suspecting she was going to despise herself for behaving in this way after he had gone. "Oh, Matt, please – you've got to believe me! I'm sorry, I'm sorry. If – if you want me—"

"No!" He raked back his hair, running a questing hand over the darkening line of his jawline. "No, Darrell, and you being a nurse must know better than that. It's just not possible, as I'm sure you're aware. You have an original approach, though, I'll give you that. Lead a guy on, break him up, and then ask to put the pieces together again! My God!" he uttered a short mirthless laugh. "That's beautiful!"

"Matt, *please* !"

"Please what?" He finished fastening his shirt, and sat down to put on his socks and shoes. "Look – let's forget it, shall we?

Put it down to experience." He shook his head. "It's an experience I want to forget, believe me!"

Darrell was crumbling inside. "You're – you're not going?"

"Aren't I? I thought I was." He finished his laces and stood up.

She made one last desperate attempt to detain him, rushing across to him and sliding her arms around his waist, pressing her face against his chest. "Oh, Matt," she breathed. "Don't hate me! Please, don't hate me!"

There was a moment when she thought she had got through to him, when his hands lingered on her shoulders and she heard his swiftly indrawn breath. But then he forced her away from him, and went past her to get his jacket from the living room. However, at the door he halted and looked back at her, his face contorted with some emotion that was tearing him apart.

"I don't *hate* you, Darrell," he muttered savagely. "I wish to God I did!"

And he wrenched open the door and went out, slamming it behind him.

CHAPTER FIVE

Darrell's mother had arranged a small dinner party for Saturday evening. This in itself would not have troubled Darrell too much in her still numbed state had not one of the guests turned out to be Barry Penrose.

"Oh, Mummy!" she exclaimed on Saturday morning, when her mother had been forced to reveal her plans. "What on earth did you ask Barry for?"

"You know why." Mrs. Anderson regarded her daughter impatiently. "He was terribly distressed when you decided to go and work in the north of England, and as you've deliberately avoided him every time you've been home, I thought it was high time you met again and made friends."

Darrell paced restlessly about the elegantly furnished lounge of her mother's house. Walls of cinnamon and chocolate brown brocade were a fitting backcloth to the honey-gold cushions and dark antique furniture. "Mummy, Barry and I have nothing to say to one another!"

"I disagree." Her mother folded her hands together, as sleek and elegant in her way as the rooms she designed. "It's obvious that this affair over Susan has upset you more than you'd care to admit, and if you want my opinion, a change of scene wouldn't come amiss."

Darrell stopped to frown at her. "You mean you think I should come back to – to London to work?"

Her mother nodded. "I think so. Apart from anything else, I see nothing of you these days."

"You didn't see a lot when I was in London," pointed out Darrell dryly.

"Maybe not." Her mother bent to pick up an exquisite ebony figurine, smoothing it between her fingers almost lovingly. "But this period you've spent in Sedgeley has made me realise that I'm not getting any younger, and that we should see more of one another than we do."

"Oh, Mummy!" Darrell stared at her helplessly. "You're forty-eight! That's hardly your dotage!"

Mrs. Anderson shrugged, putting the figurine down again. "Perhaps not. But I am a lonely woman, Darrell."

"I don't believe it!" Darrell was incredulous. "You're never at home! You never have time to be lonely! Besides," she paused, "if you feel like this, why are you pushing me into Barry's arms?"

Her mother smiled ruefully. "All right, Darrell, I give in. I felt sorry for Barry, that's all. You know how he feels about you."

"I know how I feel about him, and that's more to the point," retorted Darrell shortly. "Mummy, would you have me marry Barry Penrose knowing I'm not in love with him?"

"In love, in love!" Her mother clicked her tongue irritably. "What is love? I loved your father, and look where that got me!"

"And you think a marriage between Barry and me would work because I don't love him?"

"I didn't say that. But he is good-looking – and his father does own Penrose Plastics."

"Exactly. You think he's a good catch – financially."

"Money's important."

"Not that important."

"Without it, you can be pretty miserable. If your father had earned enough to provide adequately for all of us—"

"He did!"

"No, he didn't." Her mother held her head stiffly. "You forget, Darrell, I'd been used to better things. If all your grandfather's money hadn't had to go in death duties . . ." She moved to the mantelshelf and lifted a delicate Sèvres vase, its mazarin blue ground intricately painted in panels with chubby figures from the eighteenth century. "I have an artistic nature. I – need beautiful things around me. Your father could never appreciate this."

"Antiques!" said Darrell scornfully. "How could Daddy afford antiques?"

"Precisely." Her mother replaced the vase and turned to face her daughter. "Your father could *not* afford such things. And besides, his needs in life were purely functional – a room to live in, food to eat, and a woman to take to his bed!"

Darrell turned away, sickened by this demonstration of her mother's selfishness. "Well, anyway," she exclaimed jerkily, "you're wasting your time with me. I'm not like you. I suppose I must be more like Daddy than I imagined. The functional things would suit me fine, providing I shared them with the man I loved."

"Oh, Darrell!" Her mother made a frustrated gesture. "You're much too impractical!"

Darrell stared through the window down the road of

78

handsome, tree-screened detached houses, so different from the terraced houses in Windsor Street. Perhaps she was impractical, she thought, but the Lawfords had more wealth in their house than in the whole of Courtenay Road.

A knife turned in her stomach. How could she visit the Lawfords' home now, knowing how treacherously she had repaid their many kindnesses to her? The family might not approve of Celine, but she was Matthew's wife, and they would approve of Darrell's relationship with him even less. What if Matthew were to come home again and she was there? Could she risk the possibility that her presence might force him to stay away? She knew she could not. So where did that leave her, and what was she going to do about it?

The idea of coming back to London to work was not appealing, but she realised that Sedgeley would never be the same again. When she first went to work there, there had been Susan, and later on, all the members of that gregarious family. But Susan was dead . . .

Mrs. Anderson made a sound behind her, and then exclaimed: "Darrell, what are you brooding about?"

Darrell turned slowly. "As a matter of fact, I was wondering about what you said – about needing a change of scene."

Her mother gasped. "You don't mean you're actually considering coming back south to work?"

"I'm not sure. With Susan dead . . ." She paused. "I shall miss her terribly. Have you any objections?"

"My dear child, I never wanted you to go away. That was your idea."

"I suppose I could go back to the Princess Mary," mused Darrell thoughtfully. "Matron was quite sorry to lose me."

"Then why don't you go and see her this weekend – *today*!" suggested her mother eagerly. "I'm sure she'd love to see you."

79

Darrell's expression was tolerant as she regarded her mother. "You see this as the ideal opportunity to throw Barry and me together again, don't you?" she exclaimed.

Mrs. Anderson sighed. "Of course not. I was thinking of you, darling, that's all. Besides, there are far more suitable men in London than Barry Penrose."

Darrell thought her mother's suggestion over, but much to Mrs. Anderson's disappointment decided to wait and see how she felt once she got back to work again. It was too precipitate, making other arrangements, handing in her notice. And deep down the idea of breaking all ties with the Lawford family, and through them with Matthew, tore her to pieces.

The dinner party was a minor success. Mrs. Anderson had invited her neighbours, the Garricks, Laurence Meynell, her accountant, and Barry. Nicholas Garrick owned a string of garages in and around London, and although Darrell found his conversation rather limited, his wife, Dulcie, was secretary to a television producer, and she had a fund of anecdotes ideal for any occasion. Laurence Meynell was a bachelor in his middle fifties. From time to time, Darrell had expected her mother to announce that they were going to get married, but experience had taught her that Edwina Anderson was never likely to risk the extinguishing of her personality by another man ever again.

Barry was so patently delighted to see her again that Darrell was made guiltily aware of her own lack of enthusiasm at seeing him. Why couldn't she feel that tingling awareness of her own femininity in his presence as she did when Matthew was around? What was there about Matthew that melted her bones and aroused such a wanton longing for him inside her? Barry was just as good-looking, his clothes fitted him equally well. But his eyes were not Matthew's deep-set eyes, they did not have the same penetration, the same directness that could strip her of any defence she might raise against him. Barry didn't move like Matthew moved, Barry's fulsome compliments were not Matthew's words, and no amount of wishing could make them so.

"How long are you staying?" he asked Darrell after dinner, when they had a moment alone. "Your mother told me about Susan. I'm sorry."

Darrell glanced across at her mother talking to the Garricks. "I'm going back to Sedgeley tomorrow evening," she said.

"Tomorrow!" Barry was aghast. "Can't you stay for a few days?"

"I've been her since yesterday," Darrell pointed out quietly. "And I do have a job to do."

Barry sighed. "I see."

"I'm sorry, Barry."

"So am I." He shifted his coffee cup from one hand to the other and raised the goblet of brandy her mother had set beside him to his lips. "You haven't changed your mind, then?"

"Changed my mind?" Darrell flicked another glance towards her mother. "No. Was there any reason that you might think I had?"

Barry pushed his empty coffee cup on to a low table, and shook his head. "No. No, I guess not." He looked down at her desperately. "What's wrong with me, Darrell? What is there about me that repulses you so?"

Darrell gasped. "Nothing! Don't be silly, Barry. You don't repulse me. It's just that—"

"You said before you went away that there was no one else."

"There wasn't. There isn't." She breathed deeply. "Barry, I like you very much, but that's not enough – not for marriage."

"People marry for a lot less."

"Maybe they do. But not me."

Barry nodded resignedly. "And in the future? You don't see any change in that state of affairs?"

"How can I?"

"I don't know. People change."

"You might change."

"Me?" He made a helpless gesture. "I suppose if I say I won't you'll consider that a fitting confirmation of your argument."

"Can't we just be friends, Barry?"

Barry shrugged. "I'll always be that, Darrell."

His words, simple though they were, distressed her more than any amount of recrimination could have done. "Oh, Barry, I wish I did love you."

"That makes two of us." He spoke with forced humour. "Well – what about tomorrow morning? Could you face going for a drive? We could have a drink at one of those small country pubs like we used to do."

"All right."

Darrell saw no harm in this, but was relieved when Dulcie came to join them, thus preventing any further intimate conversation.

Her mother was pleased when Barry came to call for her on Sunday morning. Clearly, she had not given up the hope that her daughter might change her mind so far as Barry was concerned, but Darrell, thinking of Matthew, knew there was no faint chance. It was a daunting thought nevertheless that she might well remain single all her life.

The country roads were busy on this sunny June morning, but Barry had lived in Essex all his life and knew several short cuts that took them away from the honking of horns and the smell of diesel. To Darrell's relief, he confined his conversation to impersonal topics, talking about his work and a recent trip he had made to Germany. Had that scene with Matthew not been so fresh in her mind, she might well have enjoyed the outing.

They stopped just after twelve at the Swan in Chipsbury, and walked into the crowded bar lounge. Darrell recognised several faces from the old days when she and Barry had been frequent visitors here, and she was soon the centre of a crowd of people, all laughing and talking and asking her about Sedgeley. Barry pushed his way to the bar and came back with their drinks and was himself chided for his rare appearances these days. It was all easy, goodnatured banter, and Darrell was glad they had not had to sit alone and inevitably reminisce about the past.

Barry had accepted an invitation to take part in an impromptu darts tournament, and the men were moving away towards the board, leaving the girls to gossip amongst themselves, when Darrell saw Celine Lawford. She was seated on a low banquette in one corner of the crowded, smoke-fugged room, but it was unmistakably Matthew's wife. She was languidly fitting a cigarette into a long holder, and although she was alone at the moment, it was obvious from the glasses set on the table in front of her that she was merely waiting for her escort to return.

Darrell did a quick about-face, turning her back on that particular corner of the room. She looked round nervously, but there was no sign as yet of Celine's husband. There was a throng of men by the bar, he could be hidden amongst them, but as Celine already had a drink in front of her it seemed more likely that he was away for purely functional reasons.

She took deep steadying breaths. Of all the things to happen! It just wasn't fair. That they should choose this pub, and today of all days!

"Are you all right, Darrell?"

83

Janet Grant, a friend of Darrell's from her schooldays, was now regarding her rather anxiously, and Darrell forced herself to smile.

"Yes. Yes, I'm fine," she managed lightly. "Why do you ask?"

Janet frowned. "You're looking very pale, that's all." For the moment they were isolated in the group as the other girls argued over which team would win the darts tournament. She looked curiously over Darrell's shoulder. "Did you see someone you'd rather not see?"

Darrell decided to be honest. "You – might say that."

"Do I know him?"

Darrell shook her head. "I shouldn't think so. And it's not a him, it's a her."

"I see." Janet's lips twitched. "Curiouser and curiouser."

"It's not really." Darrell sighed. "It's just a – girl I know through working in Sedgeley. The girl – the girl I shared a flat with – well, her brother is married to this girl."

"And you don't want to see her."

"I don't want to see either of them."

Janet raised her eyebrows. "Which one is she? You've got me intrigued."

Darrell hesitated, and then deciding it might be useful to have an ally, she said: "She's sitting in the corner, smoking a cigarette in a holder. Blonde – I think she's wearing a tangerine-coloured dress."

Janet continued to stare over her shoulder. "Yes, I see her. Pointed face, very slim."

Darrell bent her head over her drink. "That sounds like her."

"Well, I don't want to shock your tiny mind, but the man with her is not her husband."

"*Not?*" Darrell darted a swift look over her shoulder and

84

glimpsed the thick fair hair and square neck of the man who was leaning over Celine, one hand curved round the nape of her neck. She turned back sharply, and stared at Janet. "How – how do you know it's not her husband?"

Janet shrugged, and sipped her Martini cocktail. "Simple. I know the man. His name is David Farrell, and he and his wife live a couple of houses away from my parents." She shook her head at Darrell's shocked expression. "Darling, it happens all the time. Particularly with men like David Farrell!"

"You – know – him?"

"Of course. He and Josie, that's his wife, came to live in Cedar Drive about five years ago. Since then, his name's become a common topic of conversation at coffee mornings."

"I see." Darrell absorbed this with distaste.

"Your friend's brother's wife looks well able to take care of herself," Janet went on blandly. "Now you've drawn my attention to her, I vaguely recall seeing her in here before, but not with David. What's her husband like?"

What was Matthew like?

Darrell's palms felt moist, and her tongue stuck to the roof of her mouth. "Oh – he – er – he's about thirty-three or four, tall, dark brown hair, quite good-looking . . ."

"You know him quite well, then?" Janet's tone was wry.

"I've seen him a couple of times," Darrell defended herself swiftly.

Janet studied her revealing expression with acute perception. "You know, Darrell," she said, "I don't think it was this woman with David Farrell you were afraid of meeting. It was her husband, wasn't it?"

Darrell shrugged her shoulders carelessly. "Does it matter? Actually, I'd rather not meet either of them."

Janet made a moue with her lips. "Okay. Okay, if you don't want to talk about it." She glanced towards the group around the dartboard. "Shall we join the others?"

For the remainder of the time they were in the pub, Darrell was conscious of Celine's presence above all else. From time to time, she couldn't help catching a glimpse of the couple in the corner, but they seemed totally engrossed in each other. Her feelings towards Matthew were less easily defined, and she wondered how he would feel if he knew his wife was having an affair with someone else. Was this why he had come to her? To repay Celine in kind, or because their way of life permitted such licence? And yet Matthew had said he had never been unfaithful to Celine. How could that be, unless he was unaware of her infidelities?

Then, as they were leaving and Darrell was mentally relaxing from the strain of avoiding being noticed, they practically bumped into Celine and her escort in the foyer. Darrell had been so eager to get away herself she had not noticed that Celine and the man with her were leaving too, and her expression was ludicrous when Celine greeted her with casual indifference.

"Hello, Darrell," she said, making no attempt to release the arm of the man beside her. "What a small world it is, isn't it?"

Darrell strove for speech. "Isn't it?" she managed lamely.

"Staying with your parents for a few days, are you?" Celine was already moving towards the door, and clearly the question was purely perfunctory.

"Yes," Darrell nodded helplessly.

"I may see you again, then. Goodbye."

Celine went ahead of her escort through the door, and Darrell stood stock still for a moment, feeling her knees trembling.

Barry came alongside her at that moment, and his hand at her waist propelled her outside. "Are you feeling queasy, love?" he exclaimed anxiously, feeling the quivering beneath

86

his fingers.

Darrell shook her head jerkily. "No. No, honestly, I'm all right." She shuddered again as a ripple of remembered consternation slid down her spine. "Somebody must have walked over my grave, that's all."

The morning out with Barry might not have been a success, but it convinced Darrell of one thing. Coming back to live in London and continuing to visit her old haunts was something she could not do if there was the remotest possibility that she was going to encounter Celine . . . or Matthew . . .

The first person she saw when she got back to Sedgeley was Jeff. He was hanging about outside the bus station when the bus from Leeds got in, and his face brightened considerably when he saw Darrell.

"Hey, how's that for timing?" he demanded, taking her suitcase from her unresisting fingers.

Darrell couldn't prevent a smile from lifting the corners of her mouth. There was something so wholesome and uncomplicated about Jeff. "What are you doing here?" she asked in surprise.

"Waiting for you."

Darrell raised her dark eyebrows. "How can you be? You didn't know what time I was coming back."

Jeff winked. "Thought transference."

"Jeff!"

"No, honestly, I was waiting to see if you turned up off this bus." He grinned. "But I admit, I didn't come all the way to Leeds on the offchance of meeting you."

"That's what I thought."

"I would have done if you'd asked me to." Darrell gave him an old-fashioned look, and he went on: "Seriously, though, I brought Matt through to Yedon and thought of you coming back today and here I am."

Darrell took a deep breath. "You brought – Matt – to Yedon?" she echoed. and then, gathering herself, "I mean – what was he doing in Sedgeley?"

Jeff hadn't seemed to notice her consternation, and replied: "We were honoured, weren't we? He decided to come back for the weekend." His smile robbed his words of any malice.

"I see." Darrell absorbed this news with difficulty. So Matthew had been away while Celine was meeting her boyfriend. He obviously knew nothing about it, and her heart ached for him.

"Yeah," Jeff was saying, directing her round the corner into a side where his Mini was parked, "he came up by air this time. I think he was sick of driving all this way. He has done it four times in the last week, when all's said and done."

"Yes." Darrell wondered why he had come. She would have expected him to stay away from Sedgeley until he could be sure that he would not bump into her. Unless somehow Jeff had told him that she was going away.

And then she remembered. Matthew had overheard that telephone conversation with Jeff. He had known she was going away . . .

Jeff came into the flat with her, ostensibly to ensure that she had had no unwelcome callers while she was away. It was reassuringly deserted, and she opened the windows to get rid of the faintly musty smell warm weather always created in closed rooms.

"Do you fancy coming out for a Chinese supper?" he invited after she had put her suitcase in the bedroom, and shed her shoes.

Darrell hesitated. Food was the last thing she needed right now, but Jeff had been so kind she couldn't disappoint him again. With enforced enthusiasm she put on her shoes again, and said there was nothing she could like better.

Actually, in the restaurant, over a bottle of red wine, she did relax considerably. Jeff was an entertaining companion, and he was sufficiently like Matthew to arouse sympathetic responses inside her. From time to time she found herself pretending it was Matthew, and that was when she decided it was time she went home.

Jeff kissed her goodnight at her door. The lingering kiss he had planned didn't quite come off because Darrell managed to get her key in the door and opening it backed away from him, but he didn't seem too disappointed.

"Can I call you tomorrow?" he asked, leaning against the jamb, and she sought about desperately for some way to let him down lightly.

"I – er – not tomorrow, Jeff," she said. "I shall be working again tomorrow, and I'll be exhausted tomorrow night. Leave it a few days. Let me get back into the swing of things again."

To her relief, he accepted this, and went away whistling cheerfully. Darrell closed the door and surveyed the flat miserably. Then she went into her bedroom and allowed the tears which had threatened all weekend to fall.

CHAPTER SIX

The following week passed with reasonable swiftness. Darrell worked energetically at the hospital, deliberately tiring herself out so that by the time she got back to the flat in the evenings, she was ready to tumble into bed. She realised the exhaustion she felt was not just a physical thing, but at least she was not plagued by sleeplessness. Her fellow nurses put her behaviour down to the shock of Susan's death, and Darrell did not disabuse them. After all, if Susan had still been alive, she might not have felt so isolated in her despair.

Jeff rang twice, and each time she lifted the phone she felt the faint breathlessness she had come to associate with thoughts of Matthew. But she managed to avoid communicating her disappointment to Jeff, and allowed him to persuade her to visit the family at the weekend. She had come to the conclusion that she would hurt them far more by staying away than by crediting them with a knowledge they did not possess. And besides, she was genuinely fond of Mrs. Lawford.

Saturday night at the Lawfords' house was almost like old times. Patrick was there with his wife Evelyn and her brood, and the three brothers and Penny who still lived at home. Halfway through the evening the men cleared off down to the club, leaving the women to prepare supper for when they got home.

"How was your mother, dear?" Mrs. Lawford asked Darrell, when they had a minute alone. "I expect she was glad to see you."

Darrell smiled. "I think she's trying to marry me off to a young man I knew before I came north."

"Oh! Oh, is she?" Mrs. Lawford's eyes clouded. "We'll miss you, Darrell."

"I didn't say I was agreeable," protested Darrell, half laughingly. "I just said that that was what she would like to do."

Mrs. Lawford's eyes widened. "Then you don't want to marry this young man?"

"Heavens, no!"

"I see." Mrs. Lawford's evident relief was warming. "I know our Jeff would be disappointed if you up and left Sedgeley."

Darrell looked down at her hands. This was not something she wanted to foster either.

"I'm afraid – that is – I like Jeff, Mrs. Lawford, but – well, I'll never marry him."

Mrs. Lawford sighed. "Thank you for for being honest, my dear. But I'm sure he wouldn't agree with you."

"I know." Darrell shifted restlessly. "I – perhaps I shouldn't keep coming here. If – if he thinks that – well, that I'm coming her just because of him . . ."

"Give it a little time," suggested Mrs. Lawford quietly.

"I know Jeff. He's young yet. Younger than Penny, I sometimes think, even though he is four years older. He'll realise sooner or later, you'll see."

Darrell was not so sure. She was not even sure that Mrs. Lawford had entirely given up hope of her becoming fond of her fourth son. And while the temptation to use Jeff as a substitute for Matthew was strong, it simply would not be fair – not on either of them.

On Sunday morning Darrell was awakened by a bell. For a moment she thought it was the bell on her alarm, but although she depressed the switch, the ringing went on. Frowning, she sat up in bed and blinked her eyes. The clock said half past eight, but as she wasn't due on duty until eleven-thirty that morning, she had not set the alarm. It was the doorbell, and sudden apprehension sent her out of bed, pulling on a jade green housecoat as she made for the door.

Matthew stood outside, leaning against the wall by her door, and it was obvious from the crumpled state of his clothes and the red rimming of his eyes that he had not been to bed. There was a stubble of beard on his jawline, and intense weariness in the hunching of his shoulders.

Darrell stared at him speechlessly, instantly aware of the defeated expression in his eyes. "Can I come in?" he asked flatly, and she stood aside to allow him to do so.

"Do you want some tea?" she asked jerkily, when the door was closed and Matthew was standing politely by the couch, waiting for her to ask him to sit down.

"Tea?" He nodded. "Yes, thank you. That would be very welcome."

Darrell hesitated a moment, and then indicated the couch. "Won't you sit down?"

"Thank you," he said again, and complied.

He had made no apology for calling at this time of a Sunday

morning, and Darrell could not bring herself to demand an explanation. Instead, she went to put the kettle on, running combing fingers through tangled red-gold hair. What a sight she must look, she thought, peering at her reflection in the chrome plating of the kettle – untidy hair, make-up-less face, eyes still heavy from sleep. And what on earth had he come here for?

She stayed in the kitchen while the kettle boiled, preparing a tray with deliberate slowness, putting off the moment when she would have to go back into the living room and confront him again. But when she did carry the tray through to him, she found to her dismay that he had fallen asleep. He looked particularly vulnerable lying there, his dark head against the grey upholstery, the denim shirt he was wearing under a dark blue corded jacket open to reveal the hollows of this throat. He looked thinner than she remembered, his cheekbones visible in his lean intelligent face.

She put down the tray on the low table on the hearth and knelt to pour herself some tea. Then she carried her cup to an armchair and sat down to wait for him to wake up. Whether a consciousness of being observed disturbed him, or whether he had simply just been dozing, she wasn't sure, but after about ten minutes he opened his eyes and seeing her dragged himself upright.

"God, I'm sorry," he muttered, scraping a hand over his roughening chin. He pushed back his cuff and looked at his watch. "Did I sleep long?"

"Only about a quarter of an hour," she assured him, and indicated the tray. "I'll go and make some fresh tea."

"No. No, don't bother." He shook his head and bent forward to pick up the teapot and pour some of the still steaming liquid into his cup. "This is fine, really."

She noticed that he added cream and two teaspoons of sugar

before stirring the tea. Then he drank the whole cupful thirstily and bent to pour another.

Darrell waited a moment, and then, unable to restrain the impulse, asked: "Have you been up all night?"

Matthew looked up from gulping his second cup of tea. "Yes. I left London around two and hung around outside the flat until I began to think you must be away again."

Darrell's senses tingled. "Do – does your mother know you're in Sedgeley?"

"Is that likely?" His tone was dry.

"Then what are you doing here?"

Matthew finished the tea and put the cup back onto its saucer. "I'd like to say – because I wanted to see the family or because I've got business here. But I can't," he replied steadily.

Darrell got up out of her chair and crossed the room. "Then I don't understand," she said shortly.

"Don't you?" Matthew lay back against the upholstery. "You should. I'd have thought my reasons for being here were painfully obvious."

"You – wanted to see me?" She turned to look at him.

Matthew turned his head sideways so that he could look at her over the back of the couch. "Yes. I wanted to see you."

Darrell moved her shoulders helplessly. "But why? *Why*? After – after – "

"I know." Matthew got to his feet in a single lithe movement. "After the way I behaved – after the things I said." He shook his head. "I know I'm a fool, but I had to come back."

Darrell took a step backward. "It's no use, Matt . . ."

"Why? You're not indifferent to me, I'd swear it."

94

"You know I'm not indifferent to you," she exclaimed, "but that doesn't give you the right to – to expect too much – "

Matthew heaved a sigh. "I expect nothing. I've had some time to think this over, remember, and I've decided that, if nothing else, we should be – friends."

"Friends!" Darrell spread her hands. "How can that be? You – you still believe I've – I've slept around, don't you?"

"I didn't say that."

"It's implicit in what you're saying, though, isn't it?"

Matthew smoothed his palms down the seat of his trousers. "Maybe."

Remembering Celine, Darrell felt choked. "I think you ought to go."

Matthew hesitated, and then he said: "I came back here last weekend."

"I know. Jeff told me."

"You've seen Jeff?"

She coloured. "Yes."

"When?"

"As a matter of fact, he met me after – after taking you to Yedon."

Matthew swore softly. "How convenient!"

"It wasn't arranged."

"Do you expect me to believe that?"

Darrell held up her head. "I don't have to explain my actions to you."

"No." Matthew nodded heavily. "Point conceded."

Darrell shifted impatiently, despising herself for feeling obliged to explain. "Look – Jeff is – interested in me. He has been for some time. Susan's death has – deepened that feeling, I think."

"For you?"

95

"No, not for me. You know what I mean."

"So?"

"So – we're friends." She sighed. "I can't stop going to see your mother just because – just because – "

" – just because her eldest son – her eldest *married* son is making a nuisance of himself!"

"Oh, Matt!" Darrell's lips parted.

"Well, wouldn't you put it like that?" His tone was scathing. "After all, that's why I came back here last weekend."

"To – see – me?"

Matthew nodded. "Sure. I came straight here from the airport. When you weren't here, I thought you must be at my mother's. You weren't."

"No. I was in Upminster."

"I know that now. Jeff told me. And in any case, Celine saw you, didn't she? With some other bloke?"

"Celine?" Darrell was incredulous. "You mean – she told you that?"

"That's right."

Darrell bent her head, trying to think. What game was Celine playing?

"I know about her and Farrell," Matthew said quietly. "I can see from your face that you thought I didn't."

"You – *know*?" Darrell was startled.

"Yes." Matthew shrugged. "He's not the first."

"But – but – " Darrell couldn't take it in.

"Does it upset your preconceived ideas of what a marriage should be?" His lips twisted. "Oh, yes, I can see it does. I'm sorry."

"Don't you – care?"

Matthew made a weary gesture. "Darrell, Celine and I stopped being concerned about what one another did years ago." He looked at her with that disturbingly direct stare.

96

"The difference this time is that I'm the one who is most seriously affected."

"What do you mean?"

"I mean that Celine's affairs come and go. This is my first – and my *last*!"

"You expect me to believe you when you refuse to believe me!" Darrell cried tremulously. "How do I know you haven't said this to half a dozen other women?"

Matthew closed his eyes for a moment and then opened them again. "You don't, I suppose," he agreed defeatedly.

"And in any case, if you and Celine are so – so indifferent, why don't you get a divorce?"

Matthew hunched his shoulders. "I wondered when you'd ask that."

"It's a reasonable question."

"I know." He ran a hand round the back of his neck, parting the buttons of his shirt, making her remember vividly the hardness of his body against hers. "All right, I'll try and explain . . ." He paused. "I married Celine because – well, because she was the sort of girl I thought I needed as a wife. A good background – on paper, at least – the right connections. And beautiful, I won't deny that." He shook his head. "It was all right for a few months, I suppose. We had an extended honeymoon, which Celine thoroughly enjoyed; she always enjoys spending money. Then we came back to London, and the usual social round. But my work is demanding, sometimes I work late, very late. Celine was soon bored and looking round for other distractions. Then she discovered she was pregnant."

Darrell slid her fingers inside the sleeves of her gown. This was something she had not known about. She was disturbed to find how much it meant to her.

Matthew sighed. "One night we went to a party. I was pretty

exhausted before we went out, and I guess I drank too much. Anyway, coming back we had this crash." His lips tightened. "I don't remember much about it. Celine was seriously injured, and she lost the child. I escaped with minor cuts and bruises. Later it was discovered that Celine could have no more children. She was very – upset, naturally. So was I – but for different reasons."

"And now?" Darrell was reluctant to probe, but she had to know.

"Now we live separate lives, as I've told you. Except occasionally when it's necessary to present an allied front."

"As you did at the wedding?"

"Yes. Celine didn't want to come, but I was adamant. My mother has very old-fashioned ideas about that sort of thing. The funeral? Well, by then I didn't much care what she did."

"Because of Susan?"

"Because of Susan, yes. But I had also met you. And it was – difficult – to be alone with you when Celine was around."

Darrell's breathing felt constricted. "I see."

"Do you?" He shook his head. "Have I shocked you very much?"

Darrell wrapped the folds of the housecoat closer about her. He had shocked her, but she was dismayed to discover that she had wanted to be shocked, and in exactly this way. She had wanted to hear the things he had said, and her senses ached for him to touch her. But she had to be sensible . . .

"So you – won't divorce her?" she got out unevenly.

"How can I? Oh, I know she has these affairs, but she still depends on me. Without me, I think she would – give in to – other distractions."

"What other distractions?" Now Darrell was sceptical.

Matthew moved his shoulders. "She does have other –

problems," he told her quietly. "God, don't make me go into them."

Darrell remembered the day of the wedding, and a vague half-formed realisation of what he was trying to say came to her. But then a wave of anger swept over her.

"So you intend to sacrifice your life for someone who on your own admission cares nothing for you! Oh, Matt, you expect a lot if you expect me to believe that!"

She was stricken by the sudden pain in his eyes. "If that's your opinion, then I'd better go," he said.

He turned away from her, moving towards the door, and Darrell, watching him, knew that no matter whether he was telling her the truth or otherwise, she could not let him go, not like that. She went after him, putting a tentative hand on his arm and saying: "Oh, Matt!" in a helpless, breaking voice.

Matthew turned back to her and with a muffled groan he gathered her into his arms, pressing her close against him so that she could feel his urgent response. Then he began to kiss her, long passionate kisses that opened her lips and left her weak and clinging to him. Her senses swam beneath his hands and she made no protest when he parted her gown and cupped her breasts with his hard fingers.

"I want you," he said, his voice thick with emotion, against the soft skin below her ear, and her arms slid round his neck. She could feel the hardness of his bones through his skin, more pronounced, she was sure, than they had been. Was he losing weight because of her? She ran her hands into the thickness of his hair, twining strands round her fingers and tugging softly, pulling his mouth back to hers. He was devouring her and in his arms it was possible to convince herself that what they were doing could not be wrong. If he had carried her into the bedroom then and there, she doubted whether she would have resisted him. She was on fire for him, his skin was moist beneath her probing touch, and the mingled scents of their bodies was a potent stimulant.

But in fact it was Matthew who eventually tore her arms from around his neck and breathing unsteadily put some space between them. He went to the window, standing with his back to her, and she could tell he was trying desperately to regain control of himself. Darrell shivered and wrapped her gown tightly around her, waiting apprehensively for what he was about to say.

At last he drew a deep breath and said: "I could surely use some coffee!"

"Matt?" Darrell licked her lips.

He turned then and she saw how pale he had become. "It's all right, Darrell," he said huskily. "I'll be all right. Just give me a few minutes."

"But, Matt, I— "

"It's no use, Darrell, I can't go through with it. If you are – if you haven't – oh, God! you know what I mean. I can't be the first. Not when there's no chance . . ." He bent his head.

Darrell felt an overwhelming surge of love for him. "Matt, I love you. I don't think I much care any more about anything else."

He stared at her for a few devastating seconds, and then turned away again. "Don't say things like that, Darrell!" he muttered. "Don't trust me! Just because I've let you go this time it doesn't mean that I'll always have the strength to do so."

"Maybe I don't want you to – to have that strength."

"You don't know what you're saying!" Matthew paced restlessly across the floor. Then he swung round on her. "Look – I know how you feel at this moment. I feel the same. My God, I've gone through some pretty awful hours during these past days. And standing talking about it isn't going to make it better, but at least it's the sanest thing to do. You talk about loving me – well, maybe you do. I don't know. I don't know that I'd recognise love if I saw it – or felt it. The way I feel about you – well, I know I've never felt this way about any woman before, but that doesn't mean it's love. I'm not as idealistic as you are, Darrell. I've lived a lot longer, and as you say, I'm cynical. I want you – I *need* you. But I've got to accept that one day there'll be another man in your life, someone who will love you and want to marry you – and who you'll marry!"

"*No!*" The word was torn from her.

"Yes." He was adamant.

"You're – you're saying – you're never going to see me again?" Darrell could scarcely articulate the words.

"Oh, God! No! No, I'm not saying that!" He swore angrily. "Right now, I couldn't face the idea of never seeing you again." His face twisted. "I've got to see you sometimes, Darrell, or I think I'll go out of my mind."

"Then— "

She would have gone to him, but he held her off. "Go and make the coffee, Darrell," he said emotively. "*Please!*"

With a feeling almost of helplessness, Darrell collected the tea tray and carried it through to the kitchen. While she washed the dishes and waited for the percolator to heat, she heard Matthew using the bathroom. There was something poignantly intimate about such a circumstance, particularly as after washing he came to lean against the kitchen door, watching her.

"Can I make you some breakfast?" she asked nervously, but he shook his head.

"No, thanks. I bought a sandwich at one of the service areas coming up, and it's not that long since I had dinner."

"Dinner?" Her eyes widened.

"Sure. On the plane."

"The plane?" She couldn't help her confusion.

Matthew smiled, and her heart turned over. He had a very attractive smile. "I thought you realised. I just arrived back from the States at one a.m."

"You mean – you came right here . . ." Her voice trailed away.

"After collecting the car, yes."

She shook her head, looking at him anxiously. "You must be exhausted!"

Matthew flexed his shoulder muscles. "A little," he conceded, half mockingly.

"Then why don't you – rest here? I mean – I have to be at the hospital for half past eleven, but there's no reason why you shouldn't . . ." Her voice trailed away. "I – I finish at half past five."

Matthew shook his head. "I don't think so. I suppose I'll have to go round and see the parents. If anyone happens to see the car in Sedgeley, and they haven't seen me . . ." He paused significantly. "Besides, I have to be back in London before the morning to prepare my report."

"But you can't!" Darrell was horrified.

"Why not?" He nodded beyond her to where the red light was showing on the percolator. "I think your coffee's ready."

Darrell turned back to the percolator impatiently, but when she had placed the jug on the tray, she said: "You'll kill yourself, dashing up and down from London like this!"

Matthew brushed past her to take the tray and for a moment the look in his eyes weakened her knees. "Perhaps that would be the best thing for everybody," he commented dryly, and then carried the tray through to the living room before she could reply.

When the coffee was poured, Darrell subsided on to the

couch beside him, trying to draw his gaze to hers again. "Matt, you don't mean that!" she exclaimed.

He shrugged. He had shed his jacket to wash, and the denim shirt was turned back at the wrists to reveal the hair-roughened skin of his forearms. Then he saw the anxiety in her face, and his expression softened.

"All right, I don't mean it," he agreed softly. "I'm too selfish for that. I want a lot more time with you before I'm prepared to call it a day."

"Oh, *Matt*!" Tears filled her eyes and she turned away to set her cup down on the tray.

"Anyway," he said, deliberately changing the subject, "who was the man Celine saw you with last Sunday?"

Darrell schooled her features. "Just – a friend."

"You have a lot of male friends," remarked Matthew shortly, and she sensed his impatience at this knowledge.

"Are you jealous?"

She turned to look sideways at him, and his eyes narrowed.

"You're playing with fire, Darrell," he said harshly. "Stop it!"

"What if I don't want to?"

Matthew uttered an angry ejaculation, and leaning forward pulled her across his knees. "Look," he breathed into her hair, "I've just got over one disappointment, don't force me into another."

Darrell buried her face in the hollow between the opened neck of his shirt and his chin. "Oh, Matt," she whispered, "what are we going to do?"

"We're going to behave like rational human beings," he told her, his voice slightly unsteady. "We can't go on seeing one another at all if this is continually going to happen."

Darrell had no answer for this. Her fingers probed the fastening of his shirt, separating the buttons and sliding her hand inside. She could feel the quickening beating of his heart, the pounding of his blood through his veins, the tightening of his arm around her waist. His hand came up to her throat and his thumb moved into the hollows of her ear.

"Oh, Darrell," he groaned, "do you want me to despise myself more than I do already?"

Darrell's mouth silenced his protest, and there was a wild excitement in knowing she could arouse him so easily. The shrilling of the telephone was both shocking and unfamiliar, and it was with reluctance that she slid off his knees and went to answer it. To her complete astonishment it was Barry Penrose.

"Darrell? Darrell, is that you?"

Darrell glanced over her shoulder at Matthew, and then said quickly: "Yes, of course. What do you want, Barry?"

She sensed rather than saw Matthew's instinctive stiffening, but for the moment there was nothing she could do about it.

"I'm sorry. Did I wake you?"

"No." Darrell realised she must sound impatient. "I was up."

"Oh! Oh, well, I wanted to catch you before you left for the hospital. I expect you're working today, aren't you?" He didn't wait for her reply, but went on: "Anyway, the most amazing thing has happened. I've been left a house – in Harrogate."

"Left a house . . ." Darrell couldn't take it in. "I – don't understand . . ."

"It was my aunt's – my father's sister, Aunt Beatrice. She died a few days ago. She was quite old – in her sixties, I believe. Anyway, she left me her house – in Harrogate."

Darrell endeavoured to grasp his meaning. "So?" She glanced round again at Matthew and saw to her dismay that he was on his feet now and putting on his jacket. "I mean – what does that have to do with me?"

Barry sounded exasperated. "Darrell, Harrogate is only about fifteen or twenty miles from Sedgeley, isn't it?"

"Well?"

"Well – I'll be able to come and stay at the house at weekends, don't you see? We'll be able to see something of one another again."

"Oh, Barry!" Darrell sighed. "You wouldn't like it up here."

"Why not?" He sounded hurt. "I see. You don't want to see me, that's it, isn't it?"

"Barry, we've been into all this . . ." Matthew was standing with his hands in his pockets, clearly just waiting for her to finish so that he could go. "Barry, I can't talk right now. Could you – I mean, can I ring you back?"

"All right. If you like." Barry was abrupt.

"Good. Until later, then." Darrell put down the receiver and looked helplessly at Matthew. "That was – the friend Celine saw me with last weekend."

Matthew's dark face was brooding. "You don't owe me any explanations."

"Don't I?" Darrell twisted her hands together, aware that the tension was back between them. "You don't want to know why he was ringing, then?"

"No." Matthew walked towards the door, shaking his head. But when he glanced back at her, she saw the torment in his face. "All right," he conceded heavily, "why did he ring? I gather he's coming to see you."

Darrell spread her hands. "Oh, Matt, his aunt has left him her house in Harrogate, that's all."

"So he is coming to see you." Matthew's shoulders hunched. "I'd better get going—"

"Matt, please!" she appealed. "Barry means nothing to me!"

"Perhaps I should ask what you mean to him?"

Darrell bent her head. "He – wants to marry me."

"I see."

"But I don't want to marry him!" She looked up at him desperately. "Matt, I couldn't marry him. It's you I love . . ."

Matthew half turned so that he was not looking at her. "I suppose he has no inconvenient complications in his life. No insurmountable problem to prevent the consummation of your relationship!" he said bitterly.

"Relationship? What relationship? Barry and I don't have a relationship!" Darrell took a step towards him and then halted. "Matt, Barry knows how I feel . . ."

Matthew shook his head again. "Does he? But obviously he hasn't given up hope."

"He – he doesn't know that – that there's anyone else."

Matthew turned to look at her then and his smile was scornful. But whether that scorn was directed towards her or himself, she could not be sure. "And of course, you couldn't tell him that you were involved with a *married* man, could you?"

"Was I? Involved – when I saw him?" Darrell's eyes sparkled with unshed tears. "You'd walked out on me, Matt. I wasn't to know that you would come back."

Matthew took a deep breath. "I've got to go," he said, drawing his brows together in a frown.

"Go? Go where?"

"Back to London, I think. I don't think I can face my mother and the rest of the family today. If anyone has recognised the car, I'll find an explanation later."

"You can't mean to drive back to London without a rest!"

"What else would you suggest?"

"I've told you. Stay here!"

"Oh, no." Matthew was adamant. He reached for the

106

handle, but before turning it, he said: "And I should – think seriously about – refusing this – this Barry! Sooner or later, it's bound to happen, like I said, and perhaps it would be better for both of us if it was sooner."

CHAPTER SEVEN

During the following week, Darrell found it increasingly difficult to concentrate on her work. It was no longer the panacea it had been, and her thoughts continually drifted to Matthew, wondering where he was and what he was doing – and who he was with . . . To contemplate a lifetime of this emptiness filled her with despair, and she realised that Matthew was aware of this just as much as she. Was that why he had said that one day she would get married – to someone else? To escape from the loneliness?

Once, in theatre, she was reproved by the surgeon for day dreaming while an operation was in progress, and the warning brought her to her senses. It was useless yearning for something so far out of reach, and selfish to make other people the innocent brunt of her misery.

At the end of that day, Matron sent for her, and Darrell made her way to the senior nurse's office with some misgivings. She guessed what was to come, and was scarcely prepared for it.

"Sit down, Darrell," directed Matron gently, after their initial greeting was over, her informality causing Darrell to relax a little. "I expect you're tired."

Darrell smiled. "Not really, Matron."

"No?" Matron relaxed back in her chair and eyed the girl opposite her with shrewd, assessing thoroughness. "I thought perhaps you were."

Darrell sighed. "Because of the incident in theatre this morning."

It was a statement rather than a question and Matron frowned. "You admit – you were careless."

Darrell nodded, holding up her head. "Of course. In the normal way – that is—" She broke off awkwardly and Matron inclined her head.

"Go on. You were saying . . . in the normal way . . ."

Darrell flushed. "Well, I don't know why I said that. I mean – this is the normal way, isn't it? I – I don't know what came over me."

"Don't you? Don't you indeed, Darrell? I find that hard to believe. When one of my best nurses suddenly starts behaving in a completely uncharacteristic way, there is almost always a reason for it." She paused. "Now – what is it? Trouble at home?"

"Oh, no, *no*!" Darrell stared at her wide-eyed. "I – there's no trouble."

"Darrell, something is troubling you. And I'd like to help." Matron pushed her blotter aside and rested her arms on her desk. "I realise Susan Lawford's death must have meant a great deal to you. But I thought – we thought you had got over that. Last week – why, you worked marvellously. Perhaps a little too marvellously, hmm?"

"Matron, I'm sorry for what happened in theatre this morning. I give you my word, it will never happen again."

Matron regarded her steadily. "You're sure there's nothing you want to talk about – nothing you want to tell me?"

"No, Matron. Except that I'm sorry."

"I see." Matron lay back in her chair again and folded her hands in her ample lap. "Well, I'm sorry, too. But for different reasons. I had thought you might feel you could confide in me. Still – never mind." She hesitated. "You haven't had your holidays yet, have you, Darrell?"

"No, Matron."

"Have you got – anything arranged?"

"Going away, you mean? Oh, no, not yet. I thought I might spend part of the time with my mother."

"In Upminster. Yes, a good idea." Matron picked up a pencil. "Had you any particular date planned?"

"Why, yes – in September."

"Well, I'm going to recommend that you take your holidays immediately, Darrell. Whatever you say – whatever reasons you have for feeling as you do, I think a holiday would do you good—"

"Oh, but—"

"—and I do have the patients to consider."

Darrell's cheeks flamed. "I wouldn't let you down, Matron."

"I know, Darrell." The older woman smiled. "I don't want you to let yourself down either. Do I make myself clear?"

"Is – is that final?"

"It's my recommendation," replied Matron quietly.

Darrell got to her feet. Short of going against Matron's wishes there seemed little she could do. And besides, how could she be absolutely sure it would not happen again? Depression descended like a cloud upon her.

"Is that all, Matron?" she managed tautly.

Matron sighed. "Unless there's anything more you'd like to add." Darrell shook her head, and the other woman rose to her feet. "Very well."

Darrell moved towards the door, but before she reached it, Matron's voice stopped her again. "And, Darrell—"

"Yes?" Darrell turned expectantly.

"I should use this time to work out your problems if you can. If not – then perhaps you ought to think seriously of a change of scene."

"A change of scene?"

"I feel sure this has to do with Susan Lawford in some way. Whether it's her death, or some other complication which has stemmed from it, I'm not sure. But, Darrell, we do care about you. Even if it sometimes seems that we always put the patients first."

Darrell managed to smile. "Thank you."

Matron shook her hand warmly. "Have a good holiday! Come back and see me again in two weeks from Monday."

Lesley Irving, one of her fellow nurses, expressed her sympathy when she came into the common room and found Darrell putting all her belongings into a shoulder bag.

"I heard about – well, about old Mahendra's warning. He had no need to report you to Matron!"

"Didn't he?" Darrell sighed. "Perhaps he did the right thing. You can't afford to make mistakes in our job."

"No, but—" Lesley lifted her shoulders helplessly. "Last week you worked all the hours God sent! You're probably tired, that's all."

Darrell forced a smile. "So – I'm going to have a rest."

"But to have to take your holidays! I mean, you could have applied for sick leave!"

Darrell fastened her bag. She had almost said that she was not sick. But she was – sick at heart.

"Well, see you two weeks on Monday, then," she said, with assumed lightness.

"Yes, see you."

Lesley smiled, and Darrell went out of the room before the other girl's sympathy could arouse the sympathetic self-pity inside her. She would not give in to that. Not here anyway.

Walking home, she tried to look on the bright side. It was only Thursday evening. She had the rest of this week and two whole weeks to pull herself together. She might go to London. She might see Matthew. After all, he had said he wanted to see her again. It was a bitter-sweet acknowledgement of the power he had over her that whatever terms he wanted her on, she would still come running.

Climbing the stairs at the flat, she had the absurd premonition that he might be waiting for her, but there had been no sign of his car outside. Nevertheless, there was always a chance, and when a man appeared at her door, her heart leapt into her throat.

"Matt—" she burst out impulsively, and then gasped. "*Barry*!"

"Hello, Darrell." Barry's lips had tightened a little at her greeting. "Were you expecting someone else?"

"Yes – *no* – that is, what are you doing here?"

Barry looked pointedly towards her door, and she fumbled for her key. As she opened the door, he said: "You said you'd ring me. When you didn't, I decided to surprise you. I had to come up anyway, to see my aunt's solicitors, and I thought I might be lucky enough to catch you off duty."

"Off duty?" Darrell stifled a gulp. "Why – yes. Oh, come in. I'm afraid it's a bit untidy, I haven't vacuumed for days." It wasn't only her hospital work that had suffered, she reflected dryly. She closed the door. "Won't you sit down? If you'll give me a minute to change, I'll make some tea."

"That won't be necessary." Barry caught her arm as she would have escaped him. "Darrell, what's the matter with you? You look – different."

"I expect I'm tired. It's been a pretty hectic week. And you haven't seen me in my uniform for quite a while, have you?" Darrell tried to brush his concern aside. "Come on, let me go. I'm hot and sticky and I need a bath."

Barry let her go reluctantly, and Darrell walked tautly into the bedroom. He wasn't like Matthew at all. Matthew would never have let her get away so easily.

"Don't be long," he called, as she was closing her bedroom door. "I'm taking you out for dinner."

Darrell opened the door again and looked at him doubtfully. "Dinner? Oh, Barry, I don't know ..."

Barry's face clouded. "I've driven all this way just to see you. You're not going to refuse me, are you?"

Darrell drew a trembling breath. "No. No, of course not. I – I shan't be long."

The water wasn't too hot and the bath she took was tepid, but at least she felt refreshed after it and more ready to face getting dressed and going out for a meal. This was a complication she had not expected. Not having returned his call, she had foolishly assumed he would telephone again at some other time. She had never dreamed he might just *appear*.

She wondered if he had identified the name she had uttered when she first saw him outside her door. Still, she consoled herself, he could not know of Matthew's existence, and it was not such an uncommon name. All the same, she would have to be more careful in future.

She wore a long dress of sprigged muslin, and draped a long white scarf about her shoulders. Barry's eyes brightened appreciatively and he complimented her on the transformation. He was not to know that the brightness of her eyes and the colour in her cheeks owed more to artifice than to good health.

"You'll have to tell me where there's a decent restaurant," he said, as he escorted her down to his car. "I expect you know this area pretty well by now."

Darrell half smiled. Barry was not to know that she could count on one hand the number of times she had dined out in Sedgeley.

"The Stag is supposed to be very good," she replied, as he joined her in the car.

"Supposed to be?" Barry glanced at her. "Don't you know?"

"The Lawfords held the funeral reception there," said Darrell steadily. "That's the only time I've ever been in the place."

Barry patted her knee. "I'm sorry. I didn't mean to be tactless."

Darrell stared deliberately through the windows. "I know you didn't."

The meal at the Stag was as good as anything Darrell had tasted in Upminster, and she was not surprised when Barry expressed his reluctant approval.

"We must come here again," he asserted. "In fact, I half wished I'd booked in here instead of at the Crown in Harrogate."

"That would have been pointless, wouldn't it?" suggested Darrell mildly. "I mean, your business is all in Harrogate, isn't it? What use would it be staying in Sedgeley?"

"I might see more of you," retorted Barry at once. He captured her hand as it lay on the table. "Darrell, I heard what you said when you came up the stairs, you know. You thought I was someone else – someone with the name of Matthew."

Darrell tried to draw her hand away, but this time he wouldn't let her. "Please, Barry," she protested. "You're hurting me."

"Who is he, Darrell?" Barry persisted. "How long have you known him? You told me there was no one else."

"There wasn't – there *isn't*!" Darrell glanced round in embarrassment. "Barry, let go of my hand. People are looking."

"Let them look." Barry was unconcerned. "Who is he, Darrell? I mean to know."

"If I tell you, will you let me go?"

"Yes."

"All right, then." Barry released her hand, and she twisted both hands together in her lap. Then she sighed. "If you must know, he's Susan's brother."

"Susan? Oh, you mean – yes, I know who you mean. Her brother?"

"Yes."

"And why might you expect to find Matthew Lawford on your doorstep?"

His use of Matthew's full name was disconcerting. "He – we're friends. I just thought you were him."

Barry looked sceptical. "Really? But Matthew Lawford's a married man. Does his wife know you're a friend of her husband's?"

"Don't be horrible, Barry!"

"Is that horrible? Why should it be? It's an innocent enough question."

"How – how do you know he's married?"

"I've met him. And his wife. He's quite a well known man in the City. I'd heard he came from the north of England. I didn't connect him with Sedgeley until just now."

Darrell rested her elbows on the table and cupped her chin on her hands. So already her slip had had repercussions. Forcing herself to speak casually, she said: "Small world, isn't it?"

"Yes, isn't it?" Barry swallowed the remainder of the wine

in his glass, surveying her over the rim. "Well, at least I know the competition."

Darrell's eyes widened in dismay. "What are you talking about?"

"Don't look so innocent, Darrell." Barry was resigned. "Friendship between a girl like you and a man like Matthew Lawford just isn't on."

"How can you say that?" She paused. "Have you – have you heard – gossip about him before?" She despised herself for asking the question, but she had to know.

"I don't have to," replied Barry steadily. "I know what his wife's like. It doesn't surprise me that he finds diversion elsewhere. She's a bitch!"

Darrell trembled slightly. Her palms were moist, and a wave of suppressed emotion swept over her, making her feel slightly sick. Her contempt for herself in probing Matthew's private affairs like this did not lessen her curiosity.

"If – if that's so," she murmured carefully, "I'm surprised he doesn't divorce her."

Barry's eyes were suddenly intent. "And marry you, I suppose."

"*No!*" Darrell's cheeks burned. "But – if they're incompatible . . ."

"He couldn't," stated Barry flatly. "Galbraiths would ruin him. They hold the purse strings."

Darrell felt chilled. "I don't think I understand . . ."

"It's simple enough. Lawford is a clever man, a *brilliant* economist, I've heard it said. He has a computer for a brain." He paused, shaking his head. "But brilliance alone isn't enough, particularly not in the close-knit community of the City. Lawford was the outsider, and he knew it. That was why he married Celine, because he knew her father would sponsor him. Oh, I agree, without his business acumen Galbraiths wouldn't be where they are today. But they're powerful now – powerful enough to withstand the loss that Lawford's sacking would undoubtedly cause."

Darrell moved her head disbelievingly from side to side. She was remembering what Celine had said to her in the kitchen of the Lawfords' house on that fateful Sunday evening when she had learned that Susan and Frank had been killed – about what had his family ever done for him? It seemed more acceptable, somehow, more real, than his explanation about the accident and Celine losing the baby. And yet, by even considering what Barry had told her, she was betraying Matthew's faith in her. But what was the truth? How could she be sure? Barry's motives for telling her this could be said to be just as suspect.

Her head began to throb dully, and she wanted nothing so much as to be alone to think this out for herself. But that was not to be.

"Hello, Darrell."

The harshly spoken words brought her head up with a start, and she stared in amazement at the two young men standing by their table. One of them she did not recognise, but the other was Jeff Lawford.

"Why – hello, Jeff," she got out jerkily. "What a – surprise!"

"Yes." Jeff's eyes were hostile as they flickered over her companion. "I didn't know you came here."

"This is my first time," explained Darrell, not knowing why but feeling guilty because Jeff had found her here, dining with Barry. "Er – you don't know Barry Penrose, do you? He's a friend from Upminster. Barry, this is Jeff Lawford, Susan's brother."

Barry got politely to his feet. "Another brother," he commented, inclining his head and leaving Jeff to puzzle that one out. They shook hands with a distinct lack of enthusiasm. "How do you do, Jeff."

Jeff shook hands, silently assessing the other man, and then returned his attention to Darrell. "I've phoned twice this week, but you weren't answering. Now I know why."

"I couldn't have been in, Jeff," protested Darrell. "I've been working different hours, and Barry only arrived in Sedgeley a few hours ago."

"Hmm." Jeff was unconvinced. He made no attempt to introduce the young man who was with him, and he stood looking round awkwardly, clearly impatient for Jeff to finish. "Are you doing anything tomorrow evening? I have two tickets for the Freewheelers concert."

The Freewheelers were a folk group currently doing well in the pop music charts. Darrell had heard of them, but they were not really her kind of group. Nevertheless, in the circumstances, she decided it might be politic to agree to go out with Jeff in Barry's presence. That way he might be distracted from Matthew Lawford. It might also serve the secondary purpose of showing Barry he was wasting his time with her.

Summoning a smile, she said: "It might be fun. What time does it begin?"

She sensed Barry's impatience now, and wondered why life was suddenly so complicated. If she had never had problems with Barry, she might never have come to Sedgeley, and if she had not . . .

"I'll pick you up at seven," said Jeff, looking distinctly more cheerful, and casting a somewhat triumphant look in Barry's direction. He nodded to the man with him that they were leaving. "See you tomorrow, then, Darrell."

Darrell nodded, and Barry resumed his seat. "What was all that about?" he asked shortly.

Darrell shrugged. "You heard what was said."

"Do I take it that more than one of the Lawford brothers is in the running?"

"Oh, Barry, stop it! Look – I like all the Lawfords, female as well as male. They're – they've been like a family to me ever since I came to Sedgeley. I'm very fond of them. That's all there is to it."

"Forgive me if I find that hard to believe." Barry summoned the waiter and ordered more coffee. "Would you like a liqueur?"

Darrell shook her head, so he ordered a brandy and then lay back in his chair. "Well, whatever the case, you're wasting your time with Matthew Lawford."

"Do you think I don't know that?"

The words were almost involuntary, and as soon as they were spoken Darrell wished she could retract them. But Barry merely sighed and leaned towards her again, across the table.

"Darrell, listen to me. You and I – we could make a go of it, I know it. Oh, I remember what you said, you're not in love with me and all that, but is love that important?"

"How can you ask that?"

"Let me finish. I want us to be completely frank with one another. I appreciate that you don't want to talk about Lawford. That's understandable. But if you are involved with him – innocently or otherwise – then surely you can see that any ambitions in that direction are doomed to failure!"

"Barry—"

"Please! Let me go on. All I want to say is this – I'm not a poor man. You must know as well as anybody that one day I'll come into the business and have a very comfortable living for the rest of my life. My father wants me to get married. He wants to retire, and he knows that so long as I'm a bachelor he can't do it. He wants to feel I'm – settled, reliable, a responsible character. If I had a wife – children – he would feel secure in leaving the company in my hands. He knows you. He likes you. He approves of the match, and so I know does your mother. Can't you see all that we have going for us?"

"Two people can't get married just because their parents approve of the match!" she protested.

"Why not? It used to happen all the time. And there were not the divorces in those days that there are today."

"Oh, Barry, don't bring out that old potato! There were not the divorces in those days because it wasn't so easy to come by, and one person could always prevent the other from getting a divorce if they wanted one. In any case, people were not informed as they are today. They did as they were told, the women anyway, poor things. Thank goodness those days are over!"

"There speaks the liberationist!" commented Barry bitterly.

"Not at all. It's common sense. Women should have a say in what they do. Oh, Barry, can't you see? It's no use. You and I could never make a go of it. We – we just don't see things the same way."

Barry's lips tightened. "You can be very cruel, Darrell," he said, lighting a cigarette with fumbling ineptitude, revealing his distress. Then: "So what will you do? Marry Lawford's brother because he has a look of the forbidden fruit?"

"That's a rotten thing to say!"

"Not as rotten as I could be, believe me. And people do marry for the strangest reasons, you know."

The evening had not been a success, and Darrell was glad when Barry suggested driving her home straight after dinner. At her door, he seemed poised to make another appeal, when she heard the telephone ringing inside the flat.

Immediately, her heart began to race madly, as she considered that it might conceivably be Matthew. She was mad, she thought angrily, particularly after what Barry had told her that evening, but it was useless to try and deny the excitement that even the thought of Matthew had for her.

Hoping none of this showed in her face, she inserted her key in the lock, and turned awkwardly to her escort.

"Excuse me, Barry," she murmured. "The phone . . . I'm sorry."

Barry stared at her for a few tense seconds, and then he shrugged and went back down the stairs and Darrell let herself into the flat. Slamming the door, she rushed across to the telephone and lifted the receiver.

"He – hello?"

"Darrell?" It was her mother, and Darrell slumped down on to the arm of the chair nearby. "Darrell, I just thought I'd ring and let you know that Barry is coming up to Harrogate today, so don't be surprised if you have a visitor!"

CHAPTER EIGHT

Darrell dropped her book on to the grass and stretched out lazily on the comfortable striped lounger. She lifted the dark glasses that adorned her nose and looked at her wrist watch. It was almost four o'clock and her mother had said she would be home soon after five. She sighed. This evening they were dining with the Garricks.

It was very pleasant in the garden at Courtney Road. Because these houses had been built in the days before the demand for land was at a premium, the gardens were spacious, and Darrell had spent most of her fine afternoons out here. She had deliberately forced herself to relax and after ten days she felt she was achieving her objective.

Her mother had raised no objections when Darrell had suggested spending these two weeks with her, although she had been disappointed that her daughter had refused to see anything of Barry Penrose while she was here. Gradually, she had accepted that what Darrell needed most of all was a rest, and she had given in gracefully.

After that disastrous evening out with Barry, and her subsequent outing with Jeff, Darrell had decided her most sensible course would be to avoid either of them until her feelings could be more easily defined. Barry's revelations about Matthew had aroused a certain amount of disillusion on reflection, and although it had not made any difference to her feelings for him, it had given her pause for rationality. She believed Barry, because it would have been foolish not to do so, but she also clung to the belief that there was some truth in what Matthew had told her, too.

Now Darrell swung her feet to the ground and rose, stretching her arms above her head. The action separated the cotton shirt she was wearing from her brief denim shorts, and she rubbed her bare midriff absently as she lowered her arms. She crossed the grass slowly towards the house, feeling the sun hot upon her shoulders, burning the unprotected skin at her nape. She had secured her hair on top of her head for coolness and she ran a hand round the back of her neck as she reached the paved patio area.

The tiles of the kitchen floor were cool to her bare feet as she took a can of Coke out of the refrigerator, and she thought longingly of the delights of a swimming pool on a day like this. When the doorbell rang she went to answer it with no premonition of what was to come.

She opened the door carelessly and then stared in amazement at her visitor. Matthew stood on the lower step, supporting himself against the creeper-covered arch of the porch. Compared to two teenagers passing at that moment in their vivid summer clothes, he was almost sombrely dressed, his navy pin-striped business suit, white shirt and plain dark tie contrasting sharply with their casual attire. His face was pale, too, paler than she remembered it, and she thought he didn't look at all well.

In those first few seconds she could do nothing but stare at him, and then she managed: "Hello, Matt. Are – are you coming in?"

"Are you inviting me?"

His voice was strained and she nodded jerkily, standing aside so that he could mount the remaining steps into the house. He glanced round at the cream car parked at the foot of the short drive, and then took the two steps that brought him inside. Darrell closed the door, supremely conscious of her unsophisticated appearance, of the tendrils of hair tumbling from her topknot, of her shabby shirt and scanty shorts, and bare feet.

Matthew stood silently in the hall, and she watched him nervously. She didn't know why he had come, how he had found her here, and his sombre appearance was daunting. She could hardly believe that once he had slept on her bed, held her in his arms, that once she had almost shared the intimacy of his desire.

"I understand you've been here for almost two weeks," he said at last.

Darrell nodded. "Y – yes. It's – it's my holiday."

Matthew nodded, and she glanced round helplessly.

"Er – won't you come into the lounge? I mean – can I offer you a drink, or is it too early in the day?"

Matthew remained where he was, and she halted again, hovering near the wide doors into the lounge.

"Why didn't you let me know where you were?" he demanded, in a taut voice, and her eyes widened.

"Let . . . you . . . know . . ." she faltered. "I – did you want to know?"

Matthew's fists clenched. "Don't bait me, Darrell!"

"I'm not. I just thought—" She broke off. "How did you find my address?"

"Through Allan Inter-Designs. Eventually. I have a very efficient secretary."

"Oh, I see."

Darrell digested this. She wondered what his secretary was like. Was she young and blonde? One of those super-efficient females who appeared in magazines, always looking elegant, living fast and furiously, thinking nothing of climbing into bed with any man who attracted their interest?

"She's forty-five, married, with a daughter of your age," he said wearily, as though reading her mind. "Do you really care?"

His voice had hoarsened with emotion and Darrell felt her knees go weak. Her pulses raced at the look in his eyes, and every nerve in her being cried out for her to go to him and accept the consequences. The combination was too strong for her to resist, however crazy it might be. With a little gulp she covered the space between them, reaching up with her hands and stroking his face, drawing his mouth down to meet hers.

His response was instantaneous and complete. His hands slid over the line of thigh and hip to her waist, and he lifted her bodily against him. She felt she was drowning in physical sensation, and his urgency communicated his own desperate need of her. They were hungry for one another, and feeling Matthew's clammy skin she was concerned until she realised that her skin was damp, too.

"I've missed you," he muttered, against her ear. "Oh, God! How am I ever going to let you go?"

He lowered her weight to the floor, and buried his face in the nape of her neck. She could feel him trembling, and her arms tightened around him. She felt strangely protective at that moment. But at last he lifted his head and looked down at her, holding her loosely in his arms.

"I gather we're alone in the house," he stated soberly.

"Yes. My mother won't be home until after five," she replied distinctly.

His faint smile was rueful. "Oh, Darrell, don't tell me that!" His fingers slid her shirt off her shoulders, and he bent his mouth to the creamy flesh he had exposed. Then he straightened and looked at her again. "I don't want to leave you, but I can't stay with you here. Drive with me! We could go to the coast. I know somewhere we could have dinner. Providing you can put up with these clothes."

Darrell looked up at him with troubled eyes. "Are you sure? What about Celine?"

"What about Celine?"

"Won't she – I mean, won't she wonder where you are?"

"I doubt it. I don't really much care, one way or the other."

Remembering what Barry had said made Darrell hesitate. "I – my mother and I are expected to dine with some friends this evening."

Matthew's arms fell to his sides, and Darrell felt bereft at their going. "I see. I'm sorry. I should have realised you would have other plans."

Darrell felt dreadful. The idea of dining with the Garricks when she could have been with Matthew didn't bear thinking about. And he looked so pale – so ill, almost.

"Are – are you sure you want to take me out?" she asked uncertainly. "I – someone might see us."

"So?" He was terse.

"Don't you care?"

"Not particularly." He loosened his tie and the top button of his shirt, running a hand over his hair. He looked tired, and strained, and vulnerable. Her resistance crumbled.

"All right," she agreed breathlessly. "I'll come with you. Give me time to change."

"You look fine the way you are," he protested, but she shook her head.

"At least let me put on a skirt," she insisted, and ran up the stairs as she spoke. "Go into the lounge. Sit down. Pour yourself a lager if you'd like one. There's a refrigerated compartment in the cocktail cabinet."

Matthew looked up at her. "What about your mother – and these friends you're supposed to be dining with?"

"I – I'll leave a note," replied Darrell, and disappeared into her bedroom before hesitation brought its own uncertainties.

It didn't take long to shower and change into a smocked suntop and a long cream cotton skirt. She brushed her hair and secured it with an olive green velvet Alice band, and applied the lightest of eye-shadows to her lids. A white silk shawl completed the ensemble, and she went downstairs again feeling infinitcly less unsure of herself.

Matthew was standing by the window in the lounge. He had taken up her offer of a lager, and the empty can hung from his fingers. He turned when he heard the wedge heels of her sandals crossing the parquet flooring of the hall and surveyed her with slow delibertion. Then he replaced the empty can on the cabinet, and said: "Let's go."

Darrell was conscious of Mrs. Templeton, their next door neighbour, watching them over the rhododendrons as they walked to the gate. Although she had left a note for her mother, she knew that without a doubt Mrs. Templeton would find some way of conveying the news that Darrell had left with a man she had never seen before to Mrs. Anderson.

The sleek cream automobile at the kerb was the Jaguar Jeff had once mentioned, and she raised her eyebrows admiringly.

Matthew acknowledged this with a wry smile, closing her door behind her with controlled impatience. Then he walked round the bonnet and got in beside her, shedding his jacket and tie before levering his length behind the wheel. Already he looked less tense, and Darrell was glad.

The car moved effortlessly once it was free of the restrictions of the small town, and although Matthew said little, Darrell was content. They drove to the coast, skirting the river estuary to reach a quiet stretch of sand dunes mid-way between Holland and Frinton-on-Sea.

The sun was still hot when Matthew parked the car on a grassy slope, and said: "Shall we walk for a while?"

"Mmm, let's!" Darrell was eager, opening her door and sliding out. She stood on the edge of the dunes, looking towards the sea, the breeze deliciously cool on her bare arms. Its strength tugged at her skirt, moulding the firm lines of her body and the upward thrust of her breasts.

She decided to leave her sandals in the car, and good-naturedly Matthew removed his own shoes and socks and left them there, too. Then, hand in hand, they went down to the beach, walking to the water's edge and allowing the icy ripples to curl about their toes. Somehow Matthew's arm was around her shoulders, and her arm was about his waist, and they walked idly through the shallows, sharing the beauty of the early evening. Darrell had never known the contentment she felt with Matthew, and she dreaded the moment when they would have to part and lead their separate lives again.

A stray dog came bounding along the water's edge, showering them with drops of water, and causing Darrell to gasp and jump away, trying to avoid getting soaked. In so doing, she splashed Matthew all the more and in mock retaliation he kicked water over her. She ran away from him, laughing helplessly, and for several minutes they played like children, chasing one another all over the deserted beach. But finally, Darrell sank down exhausted, and Matthew flung himself beside her.

"Your clothes!" she protested, as the sand clung to his trousers.

"I have others," he replied flatly, and then leant over her, silencing her mouth with his own.

Desire sprang between them, shaking Darrell to the core of her being. His hard body crushed hers against the sand, and she moved restlessly beneath him, suddenly wanting everything.

"It's not enough, is it?" he said, against her lips, his warm breath filling her mouth. "I don't know how much longer I can keep this up."

"So – divorce Celine," suggested Darrell huskily, and at once he drew back to look down at her scowlingly.

"You know I can't do that," he muttered. "Don't ask me!"

Darrell's blood cooled. "Because – because of the accident?"

Matthew's eyes probed hers. "Yes. Why do you ask? You *know*."

"Do I?" She propped herself up on her elbows, not looking at him, staring out to sea.

"What's that supposed to mean?" He sat upright, staring at her hard.

"Why did you marry Celine, Matt?" she asked quietly.

He hunched his shoulders, resting his elbows on his updrawn knees and linking his fingers behind the back of his neck. "We've been into all that, Darrell," he replied wearily. "I'm not proud of my reasons, but I was honest about them."

"Because Celine had the right connections."

He looked sideways at her. "What are you trying to say? That I married her for her money? Well, perhaps I did at that. But it was what she wanted too."

"You were ambitious."

He nodded. "I don't deny it."

"So isn't it true to say that if you divorced Celine – or rather allowed her to divorce you, it would mean more than a marital split?"

One of his hands was suddenly biting into her shoulder. "Who's been telling you this?" he demanded harshly.

Darrell looked at him then, trying to school her features. "Why should anyone need to tell me? Couldn't I have worked it out for myself, bearing in mind what you'd told me?"

"No." His eyes narrowed angrily, and a pulse was jerking at his temple. "You accepted what I told you before. But suddenly you have doubts. Why? What have you heard?"

"Is there anything to hear?" she exclaimed tremulously.

"Would it do any good if I were to deny it?"

"Of course—"

"Oh, don't give me that!" He got savagely to his feet, brushing the sand from his trousers with a careless hand. "Lord, and you say you love me! Thank God, I have no part of that feeble emotion!"

Darrell was frightened now. She scrambled to her feet and confronted him desperately. "You're talking as though the situation has changed!" she declared, her lips trembling. "But it hasn't, has it? I'm still here. No matter what you say, no matter what I believe, *I'm still here*! Doesn't that mean anything?"

Matthew looked down at her broodingly. "What does it mean to you?"

Darrell gulped. "It means that – that in spite of everything, I can't stop loving you – wanting you—" She broke off, pressing her hands to her hot cheeks, and his expression softened slightly.

"Nevertheless, you do have doubts, don't you?"

"Is that so unreasonable?" she cried.

He shook his head slowly. "I suppose not." He spoke heavily. "Who was your informant?"

Darrell hesitated, scuffing her toes in the sand. "He – he wasn't an informant exactly. He was – concerned for me."

Matthew's scowl returned. "The man who wants to marry you, I presume."

It was a statement and she nodded. "Yes."

"Barry something or other. Just out of interest, what is his surname?"

"Penrose. Barry Penrose."

"Penrose?" Matthew considered for a moment. "Not – Barlow Penrose – of the plastics company?"

"That's his father."

"My God!" Matthew raised his eyes heavenward for a moment. "So he considers himself competent to judge my motives for remaining Celine's husband! What did he tell you? That her father made me what I am today? That without Galbraiths' support, I would be finished in the City?"

Darrell flushed uncomfortably. "Something like that."

Matthew's lips thinned. "And you believed him?"

Darrell moved her head helplessly from side to side. "I don't know what I believe. I suppose I found it – more acceptable."

"Why? Haven't I been explicit enough for you?" His eyes were cold, like flint. "All right, if it's sensation you want, I can give it to you. Soon after we were married, I discovered that Celine was hooked – is that the right terminology? – addicted – whatever – to hard drugs—"

"Oh, *no*!"

"I'm afraid so." Matthew's face was grim. "It began in her teens with the usual introduction to cannabis at a party, and went on from there. Around the time I was introduced to her, she had just come out of a private clinic after taking the cure. I think her father had some idea that marriage might help her to adjust.''

"But—"

"After the honeymoon, I told you what happened. She got back in with the old crowd. I didn't know what was happening. How could I? I was the poor fool that had married her, that was all! Then, like I said, she got pregnant. That was when I found out. We were going to this – party.'' He paused, the lines deepening around his mouth. "She must have been in a bad way, because she got careless and I – came upon her—" He broke off, and Darrell wished there was something she could say to relieve the tension he was suffering. "I was sick – sick to my stomach. I couldn't believe it. Oh, I'd had contact with it before – no student can go through university without encountering something of the kind. But Celine was my wife, the mother of my unborn child, and I felt murderous! Believe me, I could have strangled her.'' He drew an unsteady breath. "But, naturally, I didn't. We were so-called civilised people – intelligent adult human beings, expected to think before committing some irrational act. So I went with her to the party, and I drank everything that was offered to me so that by the time we left I had no clear idea of what I was doing. The rest you know. We crashed – Celine was injured and lost the baby. They naturally discovered she was taking heroin and she was subjected to another course of treatment.''

"And you blamed yourself? When she—"

"I didn't, initially,'' he replied. "In the beginning, I was going to leave her. I didn't ever want to see her again. But she was in a bad way, and I had to. When I went to the hospital, she must have guessed how I felt, because she begged me not to leave her. She promised she'd kick the habit, for good; that she'd reform and be more domesticated;

that she'd have other children and we'd become a real family. I just wasn't interested. Any feeling I had had for Celine died the evening I found her with the syringe in her hand. But then later, she told me that after further examination the doctors had discovered that she would never be able to have another baby.

"That really hit me. I was staggered. Up until then, I'd been able to convince myself that she'd brought it on herself, that she deserved everything she got. I told myself she didn't need me. Any fool would do. But to find out that – I had been responsible for preventing her from having the family she said she wanted – that was something else."

"Oh, Matt!"

"Then her father came to see me. He was pretty shaken himself. But he loved Celine, and he asked me to reconsider my position. He said that Celine had promised that this was the end so far as drugs were concerned. He said that if I left her and she cracked up, I would be responsible. Well?" His face was bleak. "Does that sound more acceptable to you?"

"Please, Matt, try to understand how I feel . . ."

His shirt was unbuttoned and he ran his hand over the fine dark hair on his chest. "How do you think I feel?" he muttered grimly. "Knowing that you'd take Barry Penrose's word before mine!"

"That's not true!"

Darrell was vehement, taking a step towards him, reaching out and touching his midriff. She felt the strong muscles contract beneath her fingers and ran her palms upward, over his chest. She was half afraid he would repulse her, but after a moment his hands came up and covered hers, pressing them against his warm skin, his eyes darkening with suppressed passion.

"So what is the truth?" he asked tautly. "You say you love

133

me, but what does that mean? Would you leave your safe little world for me? Would you come and live with me, even if it meant travelling half across the world without a ring on your finger?"

Darrell looked up at him steadily. "I'd live with you anywhere," she said gravely. "If you asked me to."

"Oh, darling," he groaned huskily, gathering her close into his arms. He wound handfuls of her hair across her throat and over her lips, kissing her through its silky, sensuous softness. "If only I'd met you when I first came to London! How much different my life might have been!" Then he propelled her a few inches away from him, and said quietly: "All right, I'll do it. I'll ask Celine for a divorce."

"You will?" Her heart leapt suffocatingly.

He nodded. "So far as I'm aware, she hasn't touched heroin for almost five years. Perhaps that's long enough. In any event, I can't go on like this – seeing you and touching you and not – possessing you. I have to try. And if she refuses . . ." He paused. "I've been offered the chance to lecture in the States. I'd be away six months – throughout the autumn and winter. I said I'd consider it, and I have. It will mean leaving Galbraiths, temporarily at least, but they'll survive. Afterwards . . ." He halted, looking intently down at her. "Will you come with me?"

Darrell did not trust herself to speak. She merely nodded, a wave of almost uncontrollable excitement sweeping over her. She didn't really know what going to the United States with him would entail, she knew it would mean giving up her job at the Sedgeley General and stepping into the unknown, but she would be with Matthew – with the man she loved – and right now that was all that mattered.

Matthew shook his head doubtfully. "Oh, Darrell, you do realise what you're doing, don't you? If – if Celine should choose to be – awkward, if she should decide she doesn't want a divorce – "

"I'll still come. If you want me."

"If I want you . . ." A wry smile twisted his lips. "Darrell, you can have no idea how much I want you."

They walked back to where Matthew had parked the car with their arms around one another. It was a wrench even to leave that quiet stretch of beach where for a few moments they had shared a taste of paradise.

In the car, Matthew determinedly applied himself to the task of reversing on to the road again, and then he said: "You know I can't take you anywhere for dinner looking like this." He indicated his salt-stained shirt and trousers. "Does the idea of coming home with me appeal, waiting while I change, and then dining in London? I know an attractive little restaurant just off Piccadilly."

"The idea of doing anything with you appeals," she confessed honestly, and a small smile lifted the corners of his lips.

"Oh, love, I can't wait to have you with me all the time. There's so much we can do, so much I can show you, so many places I want to share with you. This trip to the States – have you ever been to America?" She shook her head, and he continued: "You'll love it. The people are so friendly. And the scenery is magnificent. I can't begin to describe its vastness, the deserts and canyons, the beauty of the Monterey peninsula! A friend of mine, Bob Lessor, lives on the peninsula. We can go and spend a few days with him, if you like."

Darrell couldn't take it all in. It was too fantastic, too wonderful! A shiver of uneasy premonition brought goose bumps out on her arms. It was too good to be true.

Her nerves returned more strongly when they turned into Lanark Square, a distinguished collection of town houses around a central area of trees and grass. She guessed this was where he and Celine lived, and panic brought a choking sensation to her throat.

"But – Celine . . ." she protested, and he cast a sideways look at her.

"If I know Celine, she is already ensconced in some discreetly lit cocktail lounge with David Farrell, or someone like him, preparing for another evening session," he told her quietly.

"But what if she's not?"

"You're not afraid of her, are you?" Matthew frowned.

Darrell shook her head. She couldn't explain to him that the thought of Celine filled her with unease, not fear. But why? Why should she feel uneasy about Celine? What could she say – or do – to radically alter the situation? Had she so little faith in Matthew that as with Barry she was afraid of hearing something she might not like?

Matthew brought the car to a halt outside a tall, white-painted house with geranium-filled window boxes providing a vivid splash of colour, and she turned to him impulsively.

"Matt. You've known for a long time about – about Celine and other men. Why did you stay with her?"

Matthew regarded her anxious face intently. "Why do *you* think?"

Darrell shook her head, looking down at her hands. "I can't begin to understand," she admitted.

"Oh, Darrell," he exclaimed. "I don't want there to be any secrets between us. And I'm trying to be honest with you, but – well, there are some things I'd rather forget." He paused. "For example, when Celine came home after the accident, I couldn't touch her." Lines of bitterness appeared beside his mouth. "I have my share of guilt, you see. But it wouldn't work. So far as Celine was concerned. I couldn't – " He broke off. "Oh, God, do you want me to draw a picture?"

"No! No!" Darrell touched his cheek wonderingly, and he turned his lips into her palm.

"So you see, you can't blame Celine for the way she behaves."

"How – how did she take it?"

Matthew shook his head. "Not well. We had terrible rows. And then – she began going out with other men, and things became – easier."

"And you? Were there other women?" Darrell felt cold.

"*No*." Matthew raked a hand through his hair. "Oh, there were times when I needed a woman, but those sort of things are easy to arrange. I – simply wasn't interested too much. There were times when I thought I'd lost the ability to sustain a relationship with a woman. And then, I met you."

Darrell stared at him adoringly. "Will she let you go, do you think?"

Matthew leant forward and implanted a firm kiss on her parted lips. "I honestly don't know. But five years is long enough for anyone to live without any love in their lives."

"And do you think – I will bring love into your life?" she asked huskily.

"You'd better believe it," he murmured, and then determinedly thrust open his door and got out, lifting his jacket, tie and briefcase from the back seat, and walking round to open her door.

An elderly woman met them in the hall of the house. It was a beautifull hall, even Darrell had to acknowledge that, panelled in a dark wood that gleamed dully in the light admitted by a circular window above the door, whose panes were stained in various colours. There was soft green carpet underfoot that spread up a fan-shaped staircase to a railed balcony, and a vase of crimson roses stood on a delicately curved pedestal at the foot of the stairs.

The elderly woman was obviously a housekeeper of some sort and she greeted Matthew politely while reserving a slightly doubtful air towards Darrell.

"Good evening, Mr. Lawford. Have you had a good day, sir?"

Her sharp eyes took in every detail of Matthew's appearance, and Darrell wondered, rather hysterically, what she deduced from his sand and sea-stained tousers. She guessed the housekeeper was used to him returning from the City looking only slightly less distinguished than when he left in the morning.

Matthew glanced half mockingly at Darrell, interpreting her thoughts, and sharing them. Then he looked at the housekeeper.

"I've had a very good day, thank you, Mrs. Verity. But as you can see, I'm slightly dishevelled. I've come home to change before taking Miss Anderson out to dinner."

"I see, sir." Mrs. Verity essayed another look in Darrell's direction. "Does Mrs. Lawford know you're dining out, sir?"

"Mrs. Lawford?" Matthew's brows drew together impatiently. "Is Mrs. Lawford here?"

Darrell's stomach muscles tightened, and a sick feeling of apprehension assailed her, as Mrs. Verity nodded her head.

"Yes, sir. She's been waiting for you to come home – "

"*Matthew!*" The voice came from above their heads, and both Darrell and Matthew looked upwards simultaneously as Celine appeared on the balcony at the head of the stairs. She looked ghastly, there was no other word for it, and Darrell, who had only seen Celine looking svelte and elegant, was shocked by the change in her. She was wearing an exotic kimono-type dressing gown, and her hair was rumpled and unkempt. Without make-up, she looked older, and Darrell stared at her in horror. What had happened? Who was responsible for this? Surely not – Matthew . . .

"Matthew, where in God's name have you been?" Celine demanded, groping her way down the stairs, holding on to the banister like a lifeline. "Do you realise what time it is? It's nearly nine o'clock! I've been waiting for you since – since – " She broke off, her gaze shifting to Darrell and narrowing. "Well, well! If it isn't Miss Do-gooder herself! What are you doing here? Offering Matthew consolation?"

"That will do, Celine." Matthew glanced helplessly at Darrell and her heart went out to him. "Are you ill? What's wrong with you? And why should you be waiting for me? Why aren't you out with Farrell, or Pickering – or any one of your regular escorts?"

Celine stared at him in dislike, her lip curling maliciously. "That's what you expected, wasn't it? You and your – girl-friend here? You expected me to be out! How dare you fetch your – your – mistress here?"

She used an epithet which until then Darrell had only heard of, never heard used, and her skin crept in horror at the ugliness of this scene.

"Darrell is not my mistress," Matthew stated coldly, but Celine went on as if she hadn't heard him, and Mrs. Verity slipped silently away.

"What were you going to do, Matthew?" Celine almost screamed the words. "Bring her here, sleep with her here? In *my* bed?"

Matthew went towards her and tried to guide her back up the stairs, but Celine shook him off violently.

"Don't touch me! Don't touch me!" she cried vehemently. "Haven't you done enough, you filthy pig! Haven't you done enough?"

"For God's sake, Celine!" Matthew's jaw was taut. He

looked at Darrell appealingly, but she wasn't looking at him. Her whole attention was concentrated on Celine, she felt mesmerised, like a rabbit before a particularly poisonous snake. "I came back here to change. I was going to take Darrell out for dinner."

"You were going to take Darrell out for dinner!" she mimicked him cruelly. "Oh, dear! And have I spoilt that? Oh, dear, Darrell, do forgive me! I wouldn't have spoiled your evening for the world!"

"Celine, I warn you – "

"You *warn* me? Oh, that's rich! That's really rich! What are you threatening me with? What can you do to me that you haven't done already?" She looked at Darrell. "I hope you realise what a charming man it is you're associating with – what a *parfait gentil* knight!"

"Celine, for God's sake! Look – I realise this is neither the time nor the place, but it you want the truth, Darrell and I – I want a divorce!"

"*A divorce*?" Celine stared at him as if she had never seen him before. "You're asking me for a divorce?"

"Yes."

Celine began to laugh then, loud hysterical laughter that echoed horribly round the panelled hall. "You want a divorce," she cried, "you want a divorce! Oh, my God, That's funny, that's *really* funny!"

Matthew clenched his fists, and then raising his hand he slapped her hard across the face. The impact of his hand had the required effect. Celine sobered at once, holding a protective hand to the reddening marks on her cheek and looking at Matthew with hurt, bewildered eyes.

"I'm sorry," he muttered harshly. "But it was the only way."

Celine sniffed, the hurt in her eyes turning to hatred.

"You – swine, Matthew," she choked. "You swine!"

Matthew ran a hand over his forehead, and went towards the stairs. "Let me pass. I'm going to change my trousers and then I'm leaving."

"Leaving?" She stared at him disbelievingly. "You can't leave me!"

"Can't I?" Matthew was icily calm. "I'm afraid I can."

"But not – not now!" Celine's belligerence turned to dismay. "Matthew, you can't, you can't leave me! I'm going to have a baby! *Your* baby!"

Darrell's lips parted in horror, and Matthew stared at Celine as if she had gone completely mad. Then he grabbed her by the shoulder and dragged her towards him. "What did you say?" he demanded savagely.

"I – I said – I'm going to have a baby," repeated Celine tremulously. "*Your* baby, Matthew."

"Don't you dare you tell such lies!" Matthew spoke through his teeth, and Darrell, watching them, was aware of the fine line that held him back from real physical violence.

"It's not a lie!" Celine's voice gained in confidence when she saw what effect this was having on Darrell. "I'm sorry, Darrell. Perhaps I was wrong. Perhaps I did jump to conclusions. I don't believe you are Matthew's mistress – *yet*. Else why did he come back here from Sedgeley on the morning after Susan's funeral and relieve his frustration on me?"

"*Celine!*"

Matthew's anguished appeal was lost on Darrell. She was remembering only too bitterly what had happened on the night of Susan's funeral. The way she had led Matthew on and then found herself incapable of going through with it. If only she had! He was a man, and only human. How much could any man take without wreaking some revenge? Her heart felt as though it was being torn to pieces and she couldn't control the sob that escaped from her lips.

At once Matthew left Celine to go to her, taking her by the shoulders and shaking her violently. "Darrell," he muttered, his voice thickening with emotion. "Oh, God, Darrell, don't believe her! I swear to God I never laid a hand on her! I haven't touched her since before the accident!"

"The accident." Darrell said the words almost involuntarily. "But – but you said Celine couldn't have any more children . . ."

"Did he tell you that?" Celine's shrill voice broke in on them. "He told me that, too. It was what he wanted me to believe. It gave him an excuse for keeping away from me. How do you like that, Darrell? He crashed the car, he broke me up, and then he couldn't bear to touch me!"

"Darrell, for God's sake!" Matthew caught her chin between his fingers. "Can you honestly believe what she's saying?"

Darrell shook her head. "I – I don't know what to believe . . ."

"Celine's not pregnant. She can't be!" exclaimed Matthew, desperately. "Can't you see – she's lying!"

"Why would I lie about a thing like that?" Celine came down the last two stairs into the hall, dragging a scrap of paper out of her pocket. She thrust the paper between Darrell and Matthew, under Darrell's nose. "Here! Look at this. Read it! It's the result of a test I had a few days ago. It's positive, can you see that? *Positive*!"

Darrell couldn't take any more. With another sob, she tore herself out of Matthew's grasp and snatching at the door dragged it open. She ran down the steps, hearing Matthew's tortured: "*Darrell*!" but ignoring it.

She stumbled and half fell as she sped across the square, but Matthew was not following her. A quick glance over her shoulder assured her that he was still standing at the top of the steps, in the doorway to his house, staring after her, his shoulders hunched in complete dejection. She went on, even while every nerve in her being cried for her to go back. What did it matter whose child Celine was expecting? She was pregnant, and there was no way she was going to let Matthew go . . .

CHAPTER NINE

Darrell lay on her back in the bed staring at the ceiling. The curtains were drawn, and the room was darkened, and she wished her mother would go away and leave her with her misery.

"But, Darrell – a *married* man! And after the agony I suffered when your father was having his affair with Delia! How could you, Darrell? How could you?"

It was three days since Darrell had run out of Matthew's house in Lanark Square, three days since she had come home to her mother's house and gone to bed and never wanted to get up again.

"Oh, please, Mummy," she begged. "Leave me alone!"

"Thank heaven for Barry anyway," her mother spoke as though Darrell had said nothing. "Without him I shouldn't have known about Matthew Lawford, should I?"

"He had no right to gossip about my affairs to you," retorted Darrell wearily.

"Gossip? To your mother? Darrell, I'm the one person who has the right to know!"

Darrell turned her face into the pillow. "All right. So now you know," she said, in a muffled voice. "Can I be alone now?"

Mrs. Anderson clicked her tongue impatiently, but there was an element of desperation in her voice as she exclaimed: "You can't lie here any longer! Darrell, it's not healthy!"

"I just want to be left alone . . ."

"But you've been alone for days!" her mother interrupted her. "Good heavens, I hate going out to work in the mornings. I – I dread to think what I might find when I come home . . ."

Darrell felt a reluctant sense of shame. Rolling on to her back again, she said: "I shan't kill myself, Mummy, if that's what you're afraid of."

"Oh, Darrell." Mrs. Anderson sat down on the side of the bed, plucking anxiously at the coverlet. "No man is worth this, believe me!"

Darrell closed her eyes. "I'd rather not talk about it."

"But you must!" Her mother sighed. "Darrell, today is Saturday. You're supposed to be starting work again on Monday . . ."

"I know that."

"But you can't begin hospital duty in this state!"

"I know that, too. I shall go and see Matron. She knew something was wrong before I left. She advised me to think seriously before going back there."

"You didn't tell me that!"

"No – well, I thought – oh, Mummy, don't go on at me. Just let me work this out in my own way." She paused. "Have there – been any telephone calls for me?"

Mrs. Anderson sighed. "Just Barry. Enquiring how you were."

145

"I see."

"Why? Are you expecting a call? From Matthew Lawford? Darrell, how could you bring him here? Mrs. Templeton couldn't wait to tell me how he had arrived, and then – and then your bedroom curtains were drawn—"

"Mummy, I got changed—"

"Try and convince Mrs. Templeton of that!"

"Mrs. Templeton's an old – " Darrell bit off an epithet, and then ran a weary hand over her forehead. "Oh, lord, what am I going to do?"

It was the first appeal she had made in her mother's presence, and Mrs. Anderson stared at her compassionately. "If you're not going back to work in Sedgeley – we could – have a holiday together."

"A holiday?" Darrell narrowed her eyes.

"Yes. Why not? I know Mr. Leonard at the travel agents. I'm sure he could fix us up with something – a cancellation, that sort of thing."

"A holiday." Darrell contemplated that possibility. And obviously out of the country. Could she bear that? Could she bear knowing that there were hundreds and hundreds of miles between her and Matthew? Could she run the risk of his trying to contact her and failing?

She made a sound of defeat. Somehow she knew Matthew would not contact her ever again. She had destroyed the tenuous link between them as drastically as if she had put a physical distance between them. And his work being what it was, there was every likelihood that he was already out of the country and many miles away from her.

She had gone over that scene in the house in Lanark Square a dozen times since she had been lying here, and it always had the power to chill her to the core of her being. It had been a terrible scene, a ghastly experience, made all the more horrifying by the knowledge of her part in it. Perhaps she should go away. Perhaps new scenes and new places would help put the affair into perspective, alleviate the mental agony she was suffering.

"Well?" Her mother jerked her back to reality. "What do you think?"

Darrell propped herself up on her elbows, frowning. "I don't know . . ." she murmured doubtfully. "I'm not very good company."

Mrs. Anderson shook her head in exasperation. "Darrell, it's for your sake we're considering the idea. I don't expect you to be brimming over with the joys of spring. I know when your father first left me, disastrous though our lives had been together, I was shattered. It took time to get over it. This – this involvement you've had with Matthew Lawford will take time too. Please God, not as long."

Darrell drew an unsteady breath. "All your sympathies are with Celine, aren't they?"

"Celine? Oh, you mean Matthew Lawford's wife? Well, she is married to him, Darrell."

"But not happily!" burst out Darrell desperately. "He – he doesn't love her."

"I suppose he's told you he loves you."

Darrell bent her head. "As a matter of fact, he hasn't."

Her mother looked astounded. "Then what is all this about?"

Darrell shook her head. "I can't explain."

"I suppose you think you love him?"

"I don't *think* it, I know it."

"Even when he's obviously let you down?" Mrs. Anderson made a frustrated gesture. "That a daughter of mine should make a fool of herself over a married man!"

"He hasn't let me down!" exclaimed Darrell tremulously. "I – I let him down."

Mrs. Anderson raised her eyes heavenward. "Oh, Darrell, this is ridiculous. You let him down, and yet you're lying here indulging yourself in a fit of self-pity!"

"It's not – self-pity . . ."

But it was, and Darrell was only just realising it.

With a stiffening of her shoulders, she went on: "All right, all right. I'll go on holiday with you. Anywhere you say. But first, I – I have to go and see the people at Sedgeley."

"Matron, you mean? And the nurses?"

"And the Lawfords," said Darrell steadily. "Mrs. Lawford has been so kind to me. She deserves an explanation."

"You mean – you'll tell her the truth?" Mrs. Anderson was horrified.

"I don't know. I – I'll think of something."

Darrell took the train to Leeds on Sunday morning, lunched at the station hotel, and then caught the bus out to Sedgeley. It was a dull day, with overcast skies that threatened rain. She went to the hospital first, but Matron was off ill, and she was obliged to make her excuses to Doctor Morrison.

"You say Matron advised you to think carefully about coming back?" he said consideringly.

"Yes." Darrell felt uncomfortable. "There were – personal reasons."

"I see." Doctor Morrison studied her pale face intently. "I must say, you don't look fit. What do you plan to do?"

"My mother wants me to take a holiday with her. After that, I'm not sure."

He doodled on the pad in front of him. "Would you like us to keep your job open for you? I can't promise anything, of course, and in matters of seniority . . ." He paused. "But I think Matron would like me to say that there's always a place for you here if you'd like to come back."

"Thank you." Darrell looked down at her hands. "But it wouldn't be fair. I – I don't know what I shall do. Right now . . ." She compressed her lips to prevent them from trembling, and the man opposite shook his head.

"Right now you're in a distinct state of nerves!" he stated harshly. "Darrell, have you seen a doctor?"

She shook her head, and he got up from his seat and came round the desk to her. He took her wrist between his fingers and consulted his watch. Then he looked into her eyes, and made her put out her tongue.

"Definitely nervous strain," he said impatiently. "You're shaking like a leaf, Darrell. I'll give you something for that."

"Yes, Doctor Morrison."

He sighed, and went back round the desk. "Susan's death must have come as a great shock to you. But life goes on, Darrell. Get out and enjoy yourself while you're young. No one knows what is round the corner."

Darrell had a taxi to take her from the hospital to Windsor Street. That was Doctor Morrison's idea. He had given her some capsules and insisted on her taking one immediately, and then suggested that she ought not to chance travelling on public transport until it had had time to work.

It was almost five o'clock when Darrell knocked at the Lawfords' door, and her palms were moist as she linked her hands together and waited for someone to answer. It was Penny who eventually opened the door, and she smiled warmly when she saw Darrell.

"Hey! Come in!" she exclaimed. "We didn't expect to see you until later in the week. Have you just got back?"

Darrell forced a smile. "Yes – and no."

"Who is it, Penny?" Mrs. Lawford came bustling into the hall as Darrell was shedding the jacket of her trouser suit.

"Oh, it's you, Darrell. Hello, my dear. How nice to see you. You're just in time for tea."

"Oh, no, really . . ." began Darrell awkwardly, but Mrs. Lawford wouldn't listen to any protest, and Darrell was drawn into the lounge where several members of the family were sitting watching the television.

Jeff was there, and his face brightened considerably. He got up to speak to her, and Mr. Lawford waved a greeting from his chair by the hearth.

"Long time, no see," murmured Jeff, successfully annexing her in a corner. "How about the pictures later?"

"I'm afraid I can't, Jeff." Darrell was apologetic, half wondering whether she had done the right thing in coming here. "I – er – I'm going back to London in the morning."

"Going back to London?" Jeff sounded hurt. "What do you mean? I thought you'd had your holiday."

"I have. That is – I – I may be leaving Sedgeley."

"But why? What's happened?" Jeff's eyes narrowed suddenly. "This bloke in London – Barry what's his name. Is it him? Are you going back to be near him?"

"Oh, no – no!" Darrell tried to wriggle past him to speak to Mrs. Lawford. "Jeff, it's nothing to do with – with anyone. I – I just need a rest, that's all."

"You're coming back, then?" Jeff sounded less aggressive. He studied her face. "Yes, you do look rather pale, now I come to notice it. What's wrong? Had too many late nights these past two weeks?"

"Jeff, I want to speak to your mother," she said desperately. "Will you let me past? I don't have all that much time."

Jeff sighed and stood aside. "Okay. But I'm taking you home, remember."

Darrell didn't answer this. Mrs. Lawford had disappeared,

probably out to the kitchen, and excusing herself, Darrell went after her.

As she had expected, Mrs. Lawford was in the kitchen, making sandwiches, and Penny was helping her. Darrell looked frustratedly at the younger girl, and then said: "Penny, would you mind leaving us for a minute? There's something I have to tell your mother."

Penny raised her eyebrows, but her mother said: "Yes, you go along, Penny. Darrell can help me finish these."

When the door had closed behind her youngest daughter, Mrs. Lawford sank down into a kitchen chair and indicated that Darrell should do likewise. "Now," she said, and there were lines of strain around her eyes and mouth as there had been when Susan was killed. "It's to do with our Matt, isn't it?"

Darrell's face flamed. She couldn't help it. Mrs. Lawford's words were so unexpected.

"You don't have to tell me, I know," went on Matthew's mother heavily. "He's my son, remember. I've known him a great number of years, and while I know he's been living in London for some time now and his ways aren't our ways any more, he's still our Matt, and I *know* him. Coming up here every weekend like he has! That's not been his way. Lordy, before our Susan's wedding, I doubt we'd seen him half a dozen times in nearly as many years. He wasn't happy, see, and he wouldn't come here pouring out his troubles like some I could mention. No, he kept away, buried himself in his work, spent months abroad in all these exotic places like Hong Kong and Tokyo... Earlier on this year he was in Australia for three months." She paused. "But that's beside the point, isn't it? It was you he came to see, wasn't it?"

Darrell shifted uncomfortably. "I'm sorry, Mrs. Lawford —"

"Sorry? Sorry? What's all this sorry business? You've

nothing to be sorry about. You didn't make the running, I could see that. Taking you home every chance he could get; coming all this way to see you!" Mrs. Lawford sighed. "Well, love, does that make it any easier for you?"

Darrell shook her head. "There's so much you don't know, Mrs. Lawford."

"I know our Matt. He can be persuasive." She paused. "Eh, you're not pregnant, are you?"

Darrell caught her breath, shaking her head again. "No."

"Thank the Lord for that!" Mrs. Lawford looked relieved. "Well, love? What is it you want to say to me?"

Darrell hardly knew how to begin even now. "I – I'm going back to London – to Upminster. To stay with my mother for a while."

"You're not well, I can see that. That was why I thought . . ." Mrs. Lawford broke off significantly. "Is this to be near our Matt?"

"*No!*" Darrell spoke vehemently. "No." She tried to keep calm. "I – well, I've been advised to rest. I'm a bit strung up, you know how it is. My mother and I – we're thinking of taking a holiday. A – change of scene might do me good."

"Does Matt know about this?"

"No." Darrell licked her lips. "Matt and I – well, we're through, finished. He – he's married, and that's that."

"Celine won't let him go, I suppose." Mrs. Lawford's lips were tight. "Selfish bitch!"

"Oh, please . . ." Darrell couldn't bring herself to tell Matthew's mother about the baby. "It's over. Over." She hesitated. "I wanted – to see you. To tell you about – going back south. I couldn't just – go."

Mrs. Lawford patted her hand. "That was thoughtful of you, dear. Particularly . . ." She sighed, staring blindly into space. Then she focussed on Darrell again. "He – he did tell you about – about the accident?"

Darrell nodded. "Yes."

"He should never have married her, never! No matter what inducements her father offered. He was a fool!" She paused. "But he was young – and ambitious. Never be ambitious, Darrell. It doesn't pay."

Remembering her mother's vaunted ambition and what it had done to her marriage, Darrell knew she was right.

"So – you won't forget all about us, will you?" Mrs. Lawford asked anxiously. "You'll come and see us some time, won't you?"

Darrell lifted her shoulders helplessly. "I'll let you know what I decide to do," she promised.

She stayed and had tea with the family, dreading the moment when Jeff would drive her back to the flat and she would have to find some excuse to give him. But Mrs. Lawford appreciated her feelings, and insisted that Mr. Lawford should be given the task of taking Darrell home.

"You promised to meet young Brian tonight," she told Jeff firmly, ignoring his protest. "Darrell's not feeling very well. She doesn't want you making a nuisance of yourself!"

It was harsh, but Darrell was glad of her understanding. And Mr. Lawford seemed to understand, too.

"We'll be seeing you again," he said, when he dropped her at the flat. "I'm sure of it. Look after yourself."

"I will." Darrell had a lump in her throat. "And – and thank you. Thank you all."

Corfu in July was hot and busy, but fortunately not as crowded as Darrell had expected. She and her mother were staying at a hotel on the western coast of the island, and she had spent almost every day since their arrival a week ago lying by the swimming pool when she wasn't actually in the water itself. Below the cliffs where the hotel was situated, the sea was an incredible greeny-blue, and several times she had gone down the stone steps to swim in its silky depths. The hotel was full of holidaymakers, lots of them from England, but most were family parties and she had not had to fend off too many would-be admirers. Her mother on the other hand had become friendly with a middle-aged professor, holidaying alone, on the day after their arrival, and as he had hired a car for the duration of his stay. Mrs. Anderson was often out with him. To begin with, she had been doubtful about leaving Darrell on her own, but when it had become apparent that all Darrell wanted to do was lie and sunbathe, or read one of the paperbacks she had brought with her, she had started accepting his invitations. Darrell for her part was glad. She knew she was still very poor company for anyone.

But today, Darrell had accompanied them to Corfu town and while her mother and the professor sat drinking Turkish coffee on the Esplanade, she wandered up and down the narrow streets, resisting the tempting souvenirs offered her by a dozen dark-eyed vendors. The barter system was still very much in operation here, and she wondered rather cynically whether tourists really believed they were getting a bargain when they succeeded in beating a price down, and not simply the price at which the item should first have been offered. Whatever the case, there were plenty of people willing to take the chance, and Darrell couldn't help admiring the muslin shirts and caftans embroidered in typically colourful fashion.

Some paperbacks outside a newsagents store attracted her attention. They were a mixture of English, French and American editions, obviously put there to attract the tourist's eye. She was flicking through the pages of a recent best-seller when she saw that the store also sold English newspapers. They were the previous day's papers, of course, but she had a sudden nostalgia to read about things and people from back home. She bought the *Express* and the *Mail*, reading the headlines about some new strike with a grimace. Then she strolled back to where her mother and the professor were waiting, glancing carelessly down the front pages. The words danced before her eyes in the brilliant sunlight, but a small photograph towards the bottom of the page was still recognisable. She found herself staring at a picture of Celine, and immediately her legs went weak.

She had almost reached the square where at the coffee tables the political life of Corfu and the Greek mainland was a constant topic of conversation and where her mother was waiting, when sudden premonition made her stop, and draw into the shadow of the buildings to read the words below the photograph. She read them once, gasped in horror, and then read them again:

> *TYCOON'S DAUGHTER DIES*
> *Mrs. Celine Lawford, daughter of Sir Paul Galbraith, died last night in Kingstone Infirmary after a party at her home. Mrs. Lawford was the wife of Mr. Matthew Lawford, a business consultant. They had no children.*

Darrell couldn't believe it. Celine – dead! It didn't make sense. And after a party at her home! What party? Had Matthew been there? How could she have died? From what? Oh, why didn't these newspaper reports go into any details?

She read the notice again, and then folded the paper with trembling fingers and walked reluctantly back to the Esplanade. Her mother and the professor were still sitting where she had left them, but her mother had been keeping quite an intense observation on her progress towards them and she noticed at once that Darrell was pale beneath the faint tan she had acquired. Mrs. Anderson's brows drew together, and she said:

"What's the matter, Darrell? Is the heat too much for you?"

Darrell shook her head, subsiding into the rattan chair opposite and accepting the professor's offer of coffee. She didn't want to talk about the article now, not here.

"It is hot," she temporised. "Where are we having lunch?"

"I suggest we have lunch here, in town," replied her mother's escort jovially. "And then this afternoon we can visit the Achilleion."

"The Achilleion?" Darrell tried to grasp at ordinary things. "What's that?"

"The Achilleion! You know. The palace built for the Empress of Austria!"

"I don't think Darrell is particularly interested in ancient monuments right now, Robert." Mrs. Anderson was regarding her daughter worriedly. "Robert, be a dear and leave us for a few minutes, would you? I want to have a word with Darrell – in private."

The professor pursed his lips, and looking slightly put out got to his feet. "Very well, Edwina. I'll go and get some tobacco. Then perhaps when I come back we can arrange about lunch."

Darrell's mother nodded and smiled, but was obviously relieved when she and Darrell were left alone.

"Now," she said, pointing to the papers on the table in front of her daughter. "What is it? What have you read in there to take all the colour out of your cheeks? Just when you were beginning to look better, too!"

Darrell sighed, and unfolding the paper she pushed it

across to her mother. "At the bottom," she said, flatly. "*Tycoon's daughter dies.*"

Mrs. Anderson read the item swiftly, her frown deepening. "I see," she said at last, looking up. "So his wife's dead. How convenient!"

"Oh, Mummy, don't say that!" Darrell felt sick. "What do you think it means? Why is she dead?"

"Your guess is as good as mine." Mrs. Anderson looked at the date on the paper. "I expect there'll be an inquest. This is yesterday's paper, anyway."

"I know that." Darrell paused. "Will they report the result of the inquest?"

"They may do. Then again they may not." Mrs. Anderson sighed. "Sometimes people want these things kept private, Darrell. And a man in Sir Paul Galbraith's position – I should think he could keep it out of the papers if he wanted to."

"*Damn!*" Darrell shifted restlessly in her seat. "Damn."

"What does it matter? Darrell, you're well out of it, by the sound of things."

"What do you mean?"

"Well, it's obviously a – fishy situation. I mean, how old was she? Twenty-eight, twenty-nine? That's rather young to die after a party, don't you think?"

Darrell hunched her shoulders. "I have thought of that, Mummy."

"There you are, then. There may be more to this than meets the eye."

"What are you saying? That Matt may have killed her?"

"No, I'm not saying anything of the kind. But the circumstances are – peculiar."

"So what do I do?"

"What do you do?" Mrs. Anderson gasped. "What do you

mean, what do you do? What *can* you do? You stay here, of course, and finish your holiday, what do you think?" Her lips parted. "You can't be thinking that perhaps you ought to go back home!"

"It has crossed my mind," Darrell admitted.

"But why?"

"Because he may *need* me!" Darrell burst out tremulously.

"Need you?"

"Yes."

"Darrell, I forbid it. I absolutely forbid it! Don't dare to suggest such a thing. My God, it was bad enough when she was alive and you were involved with the man. It will be a hundred times worse now she's dead, and in such – well, suspicious circumstances!"

"You're only jumping to conclusions," exclaimed Darrell unsteadily. "You don't know how she died. She may have had a heart condition. Anything!" Unwillingly the thought of drugs came to her mind, but she couldn't tell her mother that! "In any case, I don't particularly care how she died. It's Matt I'm thinking of."

Her mother stared at her as though she'd suddenly taken leave of her senses. "You'd go back to England now to see a man who might well be involved in his wife's death! Darrell, you're mad! Keep away. It's nothing to do with you, thank God! Be thankful for that."

"How do I know it's nothing to do with me?" insisted Darrell, gulping. "How do I know, if Matt is responsible for her death, he didn't do it because of me?"

"Darrell! Darrell, for mercy's sake, don't even suggest such a thing! Heavens, if that were true – if this got out! It would ruin you – it would ruin *me*! Can you not see the headlines now? *Daughter of Interior Decorator Involved in Scandal of Tycoon's Daughter's Death*! It would finish me, you know that. The Galbraiths are not some penny-pinching north country family struggling to make a name for themselves in the City!"

"Would it make a difference if they were?" Darrell's lips twisted.

"Oh, stop trying to twist my words, Darrell. You know perfectly well what I mean – how much I rely on recommendation for my success. If your name became linked with Matthew Lawford's and there was a scandal – I just can't bear to think about it!"

"I don't see what interior decorating has to do with Matt," exclaimed Darrell tautly.

"No. Because you don't want to see. But you know as well as I do that the people he mixes with are the people I work for. Darrell, for pity's sake, think of someone else instead of Matthew Lawford. Think of your mother – think of your future! Think of *Daddy*!"

"Daddy? Daddy? What has Daddy got to do with this?"

"Do you think he would appreciate his name being bandied about the lecture rooms at the college? It would happen, you know. Once the press got hold of your name they'd find out everything about you – "

"Oh, stop it!" Darrell put her hands over her ears.

"I won't stop it, Darrell. You owe me some loyalty, surely."

"All right, all right." Darrell ran trembling hands over her face and down her cheeks. "I see your point."

"And?"

"I have to think."

"Here's Robert coming back. We'll talk about this later."

Darrell nodded, but deep down she knew there was nothing more to say. Her mother had convinced her that to go running to Matthew at a time like this might do more harm than good. If there was some doubt about the circumstances of Celine's death, she ought not to go to him and so provide a motive for his wanting rid of his wife. For his sake . . .

But staying on in Corfu was equally unacceptable, getting news at second hand, relying on papers for information. There might conceivably be something she could do if she was back in England. Matthew might try to get in touch with her . . .

That evening over dinner she told her mother what she intended to do.

"I'm going back," she said, waiting for the explosion, and she was not disappointed.

"You can't! I won't let you! Darrell, you can't do this to me."

"Oh, don't worry, Mummy. I'm not going to *do* anything. I'm not even going to ring Matthew up, let alone try and see him. But I have to be there, can't you at least understand that? I have to make myself available."

"Available? Available for what?"

"Available – if he wants to see me!"

"So if he chooses to drag you into this affair, you'll go. It will be his decision, not yours – or mine."

"Oh, stop dramatizing everything, Mummy! I know Matt. I know he won't – drag me into this business, if there's any reason why he shouldn't. He's not like that. He's not mean – or selfish. He – he's kind and gentle and – and I love him."

Mrs. Anderson's lips tightened. "In other words, this man means more to you than I do," she said coldly.

"Oh, Mummy, you're my mother! I love Matt. I want to be with him – always."

"Marry him, you mean?"

"If he wants me to. If not . . ."

"You'd *live* with him?"

"Yes."

Mrs. Anderson shook her head disbelievingly. "So you are

your father's daughter after all."

Darrell didn't answer this. She was her father's daughter, of course she was, but she was her mother's daughter, too, and right now that was something she would rather forget.

CHAPTER TEN

The house in Courtney Road had never seemed more silent or more empty. The occasions when Darrell had stayed here alone had been few and far between, her work and her mother's commitments almost always coinciding, but now she wandered through the elegantly furnished rooms feeling more alone than she had thought it possible to feel.

The telephone had rung, and every time she reached for the receiver she had felt a nervous trembling in her stomach, but none of the calls had been from Matthew.

Mrs. Templeton had rung from next door. She said she had been concerned when she realised that someone was living in the house when she had thought they were away, and Darrell had replied politely that she had decided to cut her holiday short. She gave no explanation, although she suspected that if her mother had revealed her mystery visitor's identity to Mrs. Templeton before they went on holiday, then she might well have guessed why Darrell had come back.

Barry rang, too. He, like Mrs. Templeton, had seen lights in the house, and he said he had not come round because it could very well have been Darrell's mother. Darrell had to accept this, but she also remembered the things Barry had told her mother about herself and Matthew, and this was a much more reasonable explanation for him staying away.

"Well, anyway," Barry went on, "I expect you've heard that Celine Lawford is dead"

That was the opportunity Darrell had been waiting for. Since her return to England, she had searched the papers religiously for news of Celine's death, but without result. Short of going to London and finding out the results of the inquest there had seemed nothing she could do, but now Barry, with his inside knowledge, seemed to present a much-needed link.

"Yes," she replied. "Do you know what happened?"

Barry was silent for a moment, then he said: "Haven't you read the papers? She died in the Infirmary after a party."

"Barry, I know that." Darrell tried to be patient. "I just – wondered if you had any – other information."

"Yes. It was pretty abrupt, wasn't it? I expect her father was responsible for that. These things get about anyway without a hungry press breathing down your neck."

"What things, Barry?"

"Well – gossip. People do, you know. Isn't that what we're doing now?"

"Barry!"

"Oh, all right. Well, your – friend's not being tried for her murder, if that's what's troubling you."

Darrell's fingers holding the receiver shook. "Barry – please! How did she die? She was so young!"

"She fell downstairs."

"Downstairs?" Darrell swallowed convulsively. "You mean,

she broke her neck?"

"No. She seemed all right afterwards, so I hear. But then she started haemorrhaging, and had to be rushed to the hospital. She died on the operating table." He paused. "She was pregnant, you know."

Darrell sank down weakly on to the arm of the chair nearest the phone. So that was it. Celine had had a miscarriage. A wave of guilt swept over her. In spite of everything Matthew had said, Celine had not been lying. She could have children – and because of Matthew's desire for her, Darrell, she was indirectly responsible for Celine's death! It was an agonising realisation. Matthew might, physically, be a free man again, but mentally neither of them could ever be free of Celine's shadow.

"Darrell? Darrell, are you all right?"

Barry sounded concerned, and Darrell forced herself to say: "Yes. Yes, I'm fine."

"I know it must have come as a shock to you," he went on sympathetically. "But I did warn you not to get involved with a man like Matthew Lawford, didn't I?"

"Oh, yes," Darrell agreed tremulously. "Oh, yes, Barry, you did your duty."

"Now, come on! Darrell, don't blame me. I've just told you what happened. It's nothing to do with me really."

"No." Darrell sighed. "No, I know it's not. Thank you, Barry, for telling me anyway. I – I wanted to know."

Barry hesitated. Then: "Are you – do you plan to go and see him?"

"No." Darrell was very certain about that.

"What will you do, then?"

Darrell shrugged, and then realised he couldn't see her. "I don't know. Look for another job, I suppose."

"You've left Sedgeley for good?" Barry obviously couldn't

believe his luck.

"I – I think so."

"Well, I can't say I'm sorry." Barry contained his excitement. "Look, how about coming out with me this evening? I mean, I know you must be pretty broken up about this Lawford fellow, but honestly, you'll get over it."

"Not tonight, Barry."

"Tomorrow night, then?"

"Give me time, Barry. Give me a few days to – to gather myself. Mummy comes home next weekend. Come for dinner on – on Sunday."

"All right." Barry satisfied himself with this. "And – and Darrell?"

"Yes."

"I still care about you, you know."

"Thanks, Barry."

Darrell replaced the receiver before she was tempted to burst into tears right there on the phone and beg him to come over and comfort her. It would have been so easy to use Barry, to pretend an affection for him she didn't feel, and while at some future date she might be forced to accept his protection, right now she needed the scourging that only a complete acceptance of her part in this affair would bring . . .

Three months later, Darrell came out of the Romford General Hospital to find Barry waiting for her. He was leaning against the bonnet of his car, and his face lit up when he saw her, slim and attractive in her dark cloak.

Three months had not passed without changes in Darrell. She was much slimmer, for one thing, and for another she had lost that inner enthusiasm which used to put such a spring in her step. Now she was just another young woman who had tasted life and found it wanting. She was more cynical, and an impenetrable shell shielded those emotions which once had been so vulnerable to hurt and disillusion.

She smiled now at Barry and allowed him to help her into the car. When he joined her inside, she said: "Have you been waiting long?"

"No. Only about fifteen minutes," replied Barry, with a grin, starting the engine. "Long enough to get cold, though. How about a drink before I take you home?"

"Like this?" Darrell indicated her uniform. "Oh, no, Barry. Take me home first and I'll change. Then I'd love a drink. And dinner, too, if you feel like treating me."

"I always feel like treating you," replied Barry warmly, and Darrell sighed.

"You're too nice to me, do you know that? I really don't deserve all this attention."

"Allow me to be the best judge of that." Barry squeezed her knee confidently. "Well, so how's the job going?"

"It's all right. It's a living."

"You used to say you loved nursing."

"I used to say a lot of things," replied Darrell quietly, and Barry realised he had said too much.

There was a car parked outside the Andersons' house in Courtney Road, a big expensive car, which Darrell soon identified as a Daimler. At once her heart began to beat a little faster. Who did her mother know who drove such a car? No one she could think of. So whose could it be?

The idea that it might be Matthew came into her head and wouldn't be dislodged. But she knew it was foolish wishful thinking. Three months had done many things—they had taught her that human nature, as imperfect as it was, could accept anything given time, that in spite of her strong ideals, had Matthew come to find her she might not have been able to resist him. They had also made her believe that this was something he would not do, and she could not go to him . . .

But now, the appearance of this car swept everything back into painful reality, and although she knew it was crazy, she could hardly wait for Barry to stop the car before she was out and running up the drive.

Barry came after her and caught her at the porch. "Whose car?" he asked, flicking a thumb towards the sleek blue Daimler.

"I don't know." Darrell's voice was breathy, but she couldn't help it.

Barry frowned as she inserted her key in the lock. "It's not Lawford's, if that's what you're thinking," he muttered harshly.

Darrell ignored him. "Damn this key!" she exclaimed, as she fumbled with the latch. "Open, can't you?"

"Give it to me!" Barry took the key from her and opened the lock without effort. "There you are!"

"Thank you."

Darrell took the key from him and slipped it back into her bag as she crossed the threshold. There were voices coming from the lounge and she walked quickly to the open doors, hardly aware of Barry closing the door and following her.

Her mother was seated on a low armchair facing a big man who was lounging on the couch. The man was easily sixty, grey-haired and overweight, but immaculately dressed in a dark suit and pale grey silk shirt. He rose to his feet at once when he saw Darrell, and nodded to the young man behind her.

"Penrose."

"Good evening, Sir Paul." Barry was tersely polite and Darrell glanced round at him in surprise. *Sir Paul*? Sir Paul – who?

Now her mother was getting up. "This is my daughter, Sir

Paul," she was saying. "Darrell – this is Sir Paul Galbraith."

Darrell's lips parted in dismay. Sir Paul Galbraith! Oh, she knew that name all right. This man was – had been – Celine's father. Was still, she supposed.

Licking her lips, she said: "How do you do?" and the big man came and took her hand.

"How do you do, Darrell," he greeted her, with a faint smile. "I'm very pleased to make your acquaintance."

Darrell, extracting her hand from both of his, looked bewilderedly towards her mother. Mrs. Anderson moved her shoulders in a slightly helpless gesture, and then said:

"Sir Paul would like to have a talk with you, Darrell. He – er – he's been waiting for the past half hour."

"A talk with me!" Darrell couldn't take this in.

"Yes, Darrell. A talk with you." Sir Paul's dark brows beetled above his strong nose. "I hope you'll give me a few minutes of your time. If—" he looked up at Barry, "if – your young man will permit me."

Barry was looking rather shocked himself, and Darrell put it down to seeing Sir Paul Galbraith here, in her mother's house.

"Come along, Barry," said Mrs. Anderson firmly. "You can come and talk to me in the kitchen."

"No." Barry was looking at Sir Paul as he spoke. "No, I'll go." He focussed on Darrell. "I'll ring you later."

"Oh, but, Barry—"

Darrell broke off awkwardly, and Sir Paul said: "That's right, Penrose. You go. Darrell can ring you later, if she wants to."

"Yes, sir."

Barry was nervously polite. He smiled apologetically at Darrell, wished Mrs. Anderson goodnight, and left them.

"Now, Darrell," began Sir Paul, and Mrs. Anderson grimaced and went out of the room, closing the door firmly behind her.

Darrell hovered near the closed doors. "I can't imagine what you have to say to me, Sir Paul," she said steadily.

"Can't you?" Sir Paul raised his eyebrows. "No, well, perhaps not."

"If it's to do with Celine, I should tell you—"

"It's not to do with Celine. At least, only indirectly." Sir Paul indicated the chair in which her mother had been sitting. "Won't you sit down? My blood pressure doesn't allow for too much standing about."

Darrell hesitated, and then she shed her cloak, and came to take the chair he indicated.

"Good. Good." Sir Paul re-seated himself, stretching his long, muscular legs with evident relief. "Now, I want to ask you something, and I want an honest answer. Do you love my son-in-law?"

Darrell had expected many things, but never this. "I – I—"

"Don't be alarmed. I'm not asking out of idle curiosity, or for reasons of revenge now that Celine is dead."

Darrell expelled her breath wearily. "I – I did love him, yes."

"Did?"

She sucked in her cheeks. "All right. Yes, I love him."

"That's what I hoped."

"You – hoped?" Darrell was hopelessly confused.

"Yes." Sir Paul felt about his person and brought out a thick cigar, holding it for silent permission. Darrell nodded, and he drew out his lighter. When it was lit to his satisfaction, he went on: "Do you know about Matthew?"

"Know? Know what?"

"I thought you didn't. Penrose didn't tell you anything, of course? I thought he hadn't when he made himself scarce."

"Barry? What could he tell me?"

"He might have told you that Matt's left the City."

"Matt's left the City?" Darrell stared at him bewilderedly. "What do you mean?"

Sir Paul sighed. "I mean exactly that. Matt's resigned from the company and left town."

Darrell shook her head. "But – but why? Where is he?"

"He's bought a broken-down shack somewhere on the Yorkshire moors, with a piece of land attached. Not far from where he used to live at Sedgeley."

Darrell couldn't take it in. "I can hardly believe it. I didn't know Matt was interested in farming."

"He isn't." Sir Paul was vehement now. "And he's wasting the talent God gave him. Matt's a mathematician, he's got a great brain! Physical things like farming mean nothing to him. He's no more at home on the land than a panther would be in a pig-sty!"

Darrell rested her elbows on her knees and cupped her face in her hands. "So – so why is he doing it?"

"Don't you know?"

"No."

"He's doing it because of you, Darrell, because of you."

"Because of me?"

"You haven't seen Matt lately. You should. I don't think you'd like what you'd see."

"How?"

"He's ill, Darrell. And I think you're responsible."

"*Me?*" Darrell was horrified. "But – I haven't seen him . . ."

Sir Paul's expression softened. "Don't you understand? That's why Matt's ill."

Darrell's face burned. "You can't be serious." She broke off, staring blindly into space. Then she looked at him again. "But why should you care?"

Sir Paul shook his head. "If you knew me better, you wouldn't ask a question like that, Darrell." He paused. "Matt's been like a son to me. I care for him deeply. He knows this, I think, but it's not enough, not now."

Darrell blinked. "Go on."

"Celine told me about you and Matthew, two days before she died."

"She did?"

"Yes. She was pretty cut up about it."

"I know." Darrell looked down at her toes.

"What do you know, Darrell? Apart from your feelings for Matt. What did he tell you about his marriage to my daughter?"

"Oh – not a lot." Darrell was embarrassed.

"Did he tell you that before they got married, Celine had been arrested for drug-taking?"

"Not – arrested, no." Darrell licked her lips. "He told me he hadn't known about it – about the drug-taking, I mean."

"No, he didn't. And that was my fault. I introduced them, Darrell. I was responsible for pushing them into marriage. I admired Matthew's drive and ambition. I wanted him for Celine's husband. I thought with a man like Matt behind her, she couldn't fail to succeed. As you probably know, I was wrong."

"Please . . ." Darrell sensed how much this was costing him to tell her this. "You don't have to tell me this."

"Oh, but I do." Sir Paul was adamant. "Without the whole story, how could I expect your help?"

"My help?"

"Yes. But first, let me go on." Sir Paul frowned. "Where was I? Oh, I know – Matthew and Celine were married. Did he tell you what happened next?"

"A little," murmured Darrell reluctantly.

"Oh, please, don't spare me. He told you about the accident, didn't he?"

"Yes."

"What did he tell you? That he found Celine injecting herself? That he went to the party they were due to attend and got drunk and crashed the car coming home?"

"That was what happened, wasn't it?"

"Fundamentally, yes. But Matt wasn't driving. That was Celine."

"What?"

"I know, I know. It was wrong of me to withhold this information, but Celine was so ill at the time and she begged me . . . She said that Matt would leave her if he ever found out, and – and she was right."

"Oh, God!"

"So the accident was all hushed up, and there was no publicity. Matt thought I did it for him. And in a way, I convinced myself that I did."

"So Matt wasn't responsible for any of it!"

"No." Sir Paul hung his head. "And there was more."

Darrell stared at him. "Celine – Celine not being able to have children?" she breathed.

"Yes. That was after. When it became apparent that Matt wasn't wearing the blame for the accident, when he told me he was leaving her anyway."

"Oh, how could you? How could you?"

"Darrell, Celine was my daughter, my only offspring! I loved her deeply. I'd have done anything for her. But now she's dead, and I can't have these things on my conscience any longer."

Darrell shook her head. "It was an awful thing to do."

"I know, I know. Afterwards, after she and Matt began to drift apart, I suggested she tell him the truth, but Celine wasn't having that. She liked feeling the injured party. If she couldn't

172

have Matt's love, she enjoyed the feeling of being able to make him squirm!"

Darrell felt sick. "Why are you telling me all this? Why now? When it's too late to do anything about it?"

"It's never too late," said Sir Paul steadily. "You say you love Matt. Go to him. Tell him so. Convince him that what I did I did from the best motives. Make his life bearable again."

"I can't."

"Why not?"

"Because – because morally I'm responsible for Celine's death, can't you see that?"

"You're morally responsible . . ." Now it was Sir Paul's turn to look confused. "Forgive me, my dear, but I don't understand you. Celine died from a haemorrhage resulting from a miscarriage. She fell down the stairs at the house. Matt wasn't even there at the time. She fell, she wasn't pushed. What possible connection can that have with you?"

Darrell got to her feet now, pacing restlessly across to the window. "I'm not without blame," she insisted dully. "The night – the night that – that Matt's sister was buried, Susan, he came to my flat. I – I was nursing in Sedgeley then. That's how I got to know him – at Susan's wedding."

"I know that."

"Well, that night, the night after Susan's funeral, Matt came to the flat. He – we – we were attracted to one another . . ."

"You made love?"

"*No!* No, I wish we had."

"What do you mean?"

"I mean – I led Matt on. I let him think I would – that we could—" She twisted her hands together. "He left me in a terrible state. He was furious – furious with me for leading him on and letting him down. Do you understand?"

"Yes, I understand. He drove straight back to London. He

was in the office at four that morning."

"Four a.m.!" Darrell took a step towards him and halted. "Four a.m.! Are you sure?"

"I should be. I spoke to him." He paused. "I should explain, my apartment is on the top floor of the office building."

"Then – then – he couldn't have . . ." Darrell drew her brows together confusedly, trying to think. "You mean, he came straight to the office – from – from my flat?"

"Judging by his appearance, I would say so. Why?"

Darrell shook her head. "But – but Celine said—" She broke off. "Do – do you know where Celine was – that night?"

"No. But knowing Celine, it would not be in her own bed."

Darrell pressed her knuckles to her lips. "Oh, *God!*"

"What is it?" Sir Paul twisted round in his seat to face her. "What did Celine tell you?"

Darrell bent her head. "She – she was pregnant when she died. She – she said it was Matt's baby. That – that the night after Susan's funeral, Matt came back and made love to her—"

"And you believed her?" Sir Paul was horrified. He got to his feet. "But didn't Matt tell you, he – he and Celine didn't *live* together?"

"Yes, but – this was something else. And Celine did say it."

"Oh, Darrell." He suddenly looked very weary. "How could a daughter of mine go so wrong? Where did I go wrong? I've asked myself that so many times." He looked at her steadily. "Darrell, Celine was more than three months pregnant at the time of her death. And Matthew had just returned from a three-month business trip to the South Pacific for his sister's wedding."

Darrell groped her way back to her chair, sinking down into it thankfully, her legs almost giving out on her. Then she looked up at Sir Paul. "So – it couldn't have been Matt's child."

"Could you believe otherwise?" Sir Paul shook his head. "It was the child of a man called Farrell, David Farrell. Celine had been having an affair with him for some months. When she found she was expecting a baby, she went to see him, to ask him to accept responsibility. Funnily enough, she seemed to want the child. Perhaps losing the baby in the crash had given her a complex or something. Anyway, Farrell washed his hands of her, told her to get an abortion! I think that was when she decided to claim Matt as its father. She told me this when she came to see me – when she revealed your involvement in the situation."

"I'm – I'm surprised she told you."

"She had to. Matt had already left her, you see."

"When?"

"Don't you know? I understand there was quite a scene."

"Oh, there was, there was!"

"There you are, then."

"Oh, Sir Paul! What am I going to do?"

"You're going to Yorkshire, I hope. You're going to talk some sense into that erstwhile son-in-law of mine. You're going to bring him back to London, and marry him with my blessing, if that's what you want."

"If it's what *I* want?" Darrell shook her head. "How do I know Matt will even *see* me, let alone anything else?"

"Because I know he can't go on much longer living the way he is doing. You'll get quite a shock when you see him. He looks pretty haggard. He's had a rough time, and I feel responsible."

"So you should." Darrell had enough spirit left to say this. "And I suppose you have no other motives for bringing him back, have you? Like taking up where he left off?"

Sir Paul nodded. "I admit – we miss him. Galbraiths miss him. But most of all, I want to clear my conscience."

"How did you find me, Sir Paul?"

"Mrs. Belding found you. Matt's secretary," he explained. "A most efficient individual."

"Yes, so Matt told me." Darrell rose now. "All right, Sir Paul, I'll go to Yorkshire. I'll see Matt. But I'm making no promises about bringing him back here. I'm not at all sure he needs you as much as you need him."

CHAPTER ELEVEN

It was late afternoon by the time the taxi from Sedgeley deposited Darrell at the foot of the track which led up to Moorfoot Farm. It had been raining, and the track was muddy, and Darrell looked ruefully at her shoes as she climbed out of the vehicle.

"Are you sure this is the place?" she asked the driver doubtfully.

"Moorfoot Farm. Yes, miss. It's up yon track. You're going to get those shoes messed up."

"So it seems. There's no – road, is there?"

"This is the only way," replied the taxi driver patiently. "D'you want to go back to Sedgeley and leave it till morning?"

"No." Darrell shook her head firmly. "No, I must go. Thank you."

She pushed a note into his hand and waved away his thanks. Then she waited until the taxi had driven away before crossing the road and opening the gate into the field through which the track to the farm seemed to lead. There was no sign of a house at the moment, but she supposed it was hidden by the rise of rough turf that made up the field.

Avoiding the muddiest spots, she made her way up the bank and drew a deep breath when she reached the top and looked down on a narrow valley with a rough-looking dwelling lying at its base. Moorfoot Farm, she thought palpitatingly, and set off to walk a little faster towards it before her courage gave out on her.

Was it only the previous afternoon that Sir Paul Galbraith had been to see her? It seemed a lot longer ago than that. But perhaps that was because the journey north had seemed endless, and she had been so impatient to reach her destination.

Her mother had been non-committal. Obviously Sir Paul's involvement had impressed her, and she had made no definite objections to Darrell's affirmation of her intentions. However, she had expressed her opinion that Darrell should not expect too much from this meeting, that Matthew might well turn her away. These were feelings Darrell shared, and as she approached the shabby buildings that made up the farmstead she wondered what she would do if he did reject her. It didn't bear thinking about.

A man in a rough woollen sweater, stained denim jeans and Wellingtons was bending over a pump in the yard that surrounded the house, directing water into an enamel bucket. He had his back to Darrell, and she could not be sure it was Matthew. Unkempt dark hair lifted in the wind, overly long now, and as he straightened and caught sight of her, her knees went weak. It was Matthew, although she could be forgiven for doubting it. A growth of beard darkened his jawline, the close-fitting jeans outlined the gauntness of his thighs and hips, and his face was thin and strained. He stared at Darrell as if she was a ghost, and then turned and walked straight into the house, ignoring her.

Trembling a little, Darrell advanced the few yards into the yard and stood hesitantly, waiting for him to come out again. But he didn't. The door banged depressingly in the wind, and somewhere a cow issued its melancholy lowing with dogged persistence.

Darrell looked all about her. The shadows of evening were lengthening, and it was much colder now that she was standing still. It was a lonely, eerie place, the wind whistling across the open moorland beyond the fells.

Stiffening her shoulders, she went to the banging door and knocked. There was no answer, and half impatiently, she pushed the door open and went inside.

She was in the kitchen of the farmhouse and at least here a fire burned in the grate and there was warmth and light. But apart from that the kitchen was barely furnished. A wooden table and chairs, a shabby velvet armchair by the fire, a rug across the hearth. Cooking was done on a calor gas stove, and the lighting came from a paraffin lamp. Of Matthew there was no sign, and she crossed the room and opened the door at the back which led into a long narrow hall.

Summoning all her courage, she called: "Matt! Matt, I know you're there. Please come and talk to me."

Silence. Her lips twitched and she pressed them together. What to do? If Matthew refused to see her, to speak to her, what would she do? Tears of self-pity welled in her eyes. She could always go back to Sedgeley on foot and spend the night with the Lawfords.

But Sedgeley was the best part of five miles away. A long distance at night, and on foot. She came back into the kitchen and looked round. Could she put the kettle on? Make some tea? At least make the effort of civility?

She was reaching for the kettle when a voice behind her said:

"What do you want?"

Darrell almost jumped out of her skin and she spun round guiltily, staring at him as if he had just appeared through the floorboards. He must have been washing – and shaving – she thought, a pang of love for him sweeping over her as she saw the jagged cut he had made with his razor on his now clean-shaven chin. He had changed the rough sweater, too, for a fine black woollen shirt, and the jeans for dark suede trousers. He had combed his hair, and she realised that its length was not unattractive. She had the almost overwhelming desire to throw herself into his arms, but something in his grim expression held her back.

"You – you've cut yourself," she said inconsequently, taking a handkerchief out of her pocket and holding it out.

He ignored it, wiping the back of his hand across his chin, smearing the blood carelessly. "I asked what you wanted?" he repeated harshly

Darrell took a deep breath. "That's rather a pointless question, isn't it? I mean – I'm hardly here to see the sights, am I?" She controlled the tremor in her voice. "I – I came to find you, as you very well must know."

"Why?"

"Why?" She raised her eyes heavenward. "Why do you suppose?"

"I don't know that I care," he muttered, his nostrils tightening. "But you should have warned me you were coming. I could have saved you the journey."

"What do you mean?"

"You're wasting your time here, Darrell. I don't want to see you. I don't want to see anybody, do you understand? Now go away and leave me alone."

Darrell's lips parted. "Matt – you don't mean that—"

"Don't I? I thought I did."

"Matt, I have to talk to you . . ."

"We have nothing to say to one another."

"Oh, we do, we do!" Darrell caught her breath. "Matt, what have you been doing to yourself? You look so - so—"

"Haggard? I know. I've already been told that."

"Who by?" Darrell paused. "Sir Paul?"

Matthew's eyes narrowed. "What do you know about Sir Paul? Oh, God, *no*! He didn't send you here to find me, did he? Oh, I knew he was determined to get me back to London, but I didn't think even he would resort to this!"

"Matt, listen to me—"

She touched his arm, but he shook her off. "Keep away from me! You're wasting your time! I've told you, I don't ever want to see you again."

"Oh, Matt, I made a mistake—"

"Too damn right! Coming here was the biggest mistake you ever made."

"No . . . no! Not coming here. About - about Celine's baby!"

Matthew's lips twisted. "Are you sure about that? How do you know I wasn't lying, like you said? What divine revelation has sparked off this sudden belief in me?"

"No divine revelation," she replied urgently. "Sir Paul told me that - that Celine was three months pregnant when she died, and - and how you were abroad . . ." She broke off. "Do you honestly believe it was that that kept me away from you?"

Matthew's face hardened. "I really don't care —"

"I don't believe that. Matt, listen to me! You *must* listen to me! I - I thought - I believed Celine, I admit it. Because - because I had to. That night - that night you left me - I could believe you might have - have—"

"Use her words," said Matthew bitterly. "That I might have relieved my frustration on her!"

181

"Well – well, all right. Is that so unreasonable?"

"Yes."

"Well, I wasn't to know that." Darrell quivered. "Matt, I didn't stay away because of that. I – I could have forgiven you that—"

"Thanks."

"Oh, Matt, don't make it so hard for me . . ." She linked and unlinked her fingers. "It was – it was the other. Celine dying of a – a miscarriage. I – I blamed myself. Can't you understand that? I – I thought – if I hadn't stopped you, if – if we had made love – you wouldn't have – she wouldn't have been pregnant. Oh, Matt, don't look at me like that. I'm only human. I – I love you so much. Please – please, believe me! Don't send me away, don't send me away . . ."

And to her ignominy, tears began to roll down her cheeks to splash unheeded on to her pale suede coat. Matthew seemed as far out of reach as ever, and the agony of it all was just too much for her.

With a little sob, she turned and fled towards the door, but he moved quicker and was there before her, blocking her exit. She turned from him, not wanting to see the contempt in his eyes when he looked at her, and then felt his hands on her arms, hard and brutally compelling, but unmistakably drawing her back against him. There was a moment when she resisted, when she half thought this was some new way he had thought of hurting her, but when her body touched his, she knew he was as emotionally aroused as she was.

With a groan, he tore the buttons of the coat open, and tugged it off her shoulders to fall unheeded to the floor. Then he twisted her round in his arms and his hungry mouth fastened on hers. There was blood on her lips from the cut which was still bleeding just above his jawline, but she didn't care. She didn't care about anything but being there in his arms, feeling his taut body straining against hers, opening her mouth beneath his and allowing him to explore the sweetness inside. His fingers slid beneath her sweater as he unfastened his shirt and brought her soft skin into contact with the rough hardness of his chest.

"Oh, Matt," she breathed, against his neck, "hold me closer, never let me go!"

"You're crazy coming here, do you know that?" he demanded against her mouth. "How the hell am I supposed to let you go?"

"I don't want you to."

"No, but dammit, I have to," he swore violently, and dragged himself away from her. Darrell made no attempt to straighten her clothes and Matthew, looking back at her over his shoulder, swore again. "For God's sake, Darrell," he muttered, "stop tormenting me! You may have expunged your guilt so far as Celine is concerned, but I haven't."

"What do you mean?" Darrell slowly pulled down her sweater, aware of her breasts pulsing with the life Matthew had pressed into them.

"Oh, God, Darrell, if I had never crashed that car and Celine had had the baby, she might not now be dead!"

"And – and would you have wanted her?"

Matthew raked a hand over his hair. "Oh, I can't answer that. I don't know. I tell myself I'd have forgotten about – about the drugs, but I don't know whether I could. But – if she'd had a baby . . ."

"It might have made no difference."

"I know that. That's what I tell myself in my more lucid moments." He nodded to the half empty bottle of whisky occupying a corner of the hearth. "Did you notice that? I never knew that so much whisky could provide so little oblivion."

"Oh, Matt!" Darrell went towards him urgently. "Matt, there's something you don't know."

"Yes, I do. Sir Paul told me. Celine was never injured in that way that prevented her from having children. He had to tell me that after – after—"

"Was that all he told you?"

"What else is there?"

Darrell stretched out a hand and touched the bloody cut on his cheek, drawing back her fingers to lick them deliberately. Matthew, watching her, was stiff and controlled.

"For God's sake, Darrell," he muttered. "What else is there?"

Darrell went close to him so that her body was almost touching his, and she had to tip back her head to look up at him. "You were not driving the car the night it crashed. That was Celine."

"What?" Matthew stared at her disbelievingly. "You're not serious!"

"I am. I expect if you probe deeply enough you could prove it, but there's really no need. Sir Paul knows the truth. It was he who suppressed it – for Celine's sake."

Matthew's hands gripped her forearms. "You mean – she was responsible . . ."

"Yes, yes!" Darrell was laughing and crying all at once at the unashamed relief in his face.

"Oh, Darrell! Darrell!" He caught her close to him then, burying his face in her neck and uttering sounds of pleasure and relief. "Oh, God! I can't believe it."

Darrell drew back her head. "Do – do you believe me?"

He nodded, his eyes heavy with emotion. "What else can I do?" he muttered thickly. "I want you too much to let you go."

"Want, Matthew?"

"What do you want me to say?" He held her head between his hands. "That I need you, that I want you, that I can't live without you?"

She nodded unsteadily, and a faint smile touched his lips.

"But there's something more, isn't there?" he asked, huskily. "You don't have to prompt me, my darling. I've learned a lot about myself these past few months. I thought I was incapable of love, but if it's not love I feel for you, then God help me, I don't know what it is that's been tearing me to pieces!"

Darrell reached up and his mouth parted hers, straining her to him, making her weakly aware of his strength and what it would mean.

When he lifted his head, she said: "Why did you come here? Are you going to stay?"

"Are you?"

"I'll stay anywhere you want me to, you know that."

Matthew shook his head half mockingly. "I bet old Galbraith didn't ask you to say that. He wants me back in London."

"I know."

"Where do you want us to live?"

"Together."

"That goes without saying." He smiled. "With or without marriage, you're not leaving me now. But I'm hoping you will marry me."

Darrell pressed her face against the hair on his chest, loving the feel and the smell of him. "I don't care where we live," she told him honestly.

Matthew sighed. "In the circumstances, I could stand going back."

"That's what you really want, isn't it?"

"No." He shook his head. "What I really want is you. And many miles between me and Galbraiths."

"The lecture tour of the States?"

"As a honeymoon? I think not." Matthew was disturbingly sensual. "That can come later."

"So you will go back to Galbraiths?"

"That can come later, too."

"And this place?"

Matthew glanced round. "It's served its purpose. Actually, though, I'd like to keep it on. Between us, we could make it quite habitable. I'm afraid I haven't bothered much for myself. Just a table and a chair, and a bed. Which reminds me . . ." His eyes caressed her. "Just how did you intend getting back to Sedgeley tonight?"

"I didn't," she replied honestly.

Dear Reader,

We at Mills & Boon are only too well aware of the burden of price increases that everyone is having to bear in the present economic situation. So we are constantly looking for new ways to make economies in the production of our books which can help us to maintain our present prices.

Nevertheless we are faced with ever-increasing costs of printing, paper and handling.

In order to avoid passing on the latest round of increases to you, the reader, we have decided to use a slightly thinner paper for our romances, beginning with the April titles. This will make only a small difference to the thickness of each paperback; there will, of course, still be a full 192 pages of romance in each book.

This small change will enable us to keep the price of our paperback romances to 30p and we hope it will help you to enjoy more of the romance reading you know you can rely on.

Yours sincerely,

MILLS & BOON

April Paperbacks

DANGEROUS FRIENDSHIP
by Anne Hampson
Before she went out to South Africa, Lena hadn't much liked the sound of her friends' daunting neighbour, Kane Westbrook. But before she had known him long she realised that her first impressions had been wrong ones, and in fact a friendship began to grow between the two of them. It was a friendship that could be dangerous . . .

PROUD STRANGER
by Rebecca Stratton
Rosalind had fallen in love with southern Italy, and was delighted when the charming Luigi Mendori offered her a job and the chance to stay on after her holiday was over. She accepted gladly—and then found that the man in charge of the new job was Luigi's far from charming brother Lucifer!

LADY IN THE LIMELIGHT
by Elizabeth Ashton
Averil supposed she ought to be thrilled at having been whisked out of obscurity to potential stardom on stage, under the guidance of the celebrated director Philip Conway —but she wasn't. Already she had been foolish enough to fall in love with him—and even if she had any reason to believe he returned her feeling, what was she to do about her engagement to John?

DARLING INFIDEL
by Violet Winspear
Young Cathy Colt just couldn't stand the autocratic Dr. Woolf Maxwell, and she didn't care in the least when her glamorous friend Tippy announced that she was going to make him fall in love with her. But someone warned Cathy, 'Beware of hate, it's first cousin to love.' Would she find out, too late, that that was perfectly true?

THE FIRE IN THE DIAMOND
by Marjorie Lewty
After years of poverty, Toni couldn't help but be pleased when she and her mother were reunited with their only relative, the rich and generous old Mr. Benjamin Warren. But Mr. Warren's business partner Gray Lawrence saw Toni as nothing but a cheap little opportunist, and didn't trouble to conceal his opinion of her. But did it really matter what Gray Lawrence thought?

30p net each
Available April 1976

April paperbacks *continued*

THE HOMEPLACE
by Janet Dailey
Her grandparents' home in Iowa had always meant so much to Cathie, and she couldn't help resenting the stranger, Rob Douglas, who had come along and bought it. But resent him or not, she certainly couldn't ignore him—and soon she found she wasn't resenting him any more. What was going to become of her engagement to Clay?

THE DANCE OF COURTSHIP
by Flora Kidd
All Cherry had to do was to fly out to Bolivia with a baby and deliver him to his relatives there. But one relative in particular, the black sheep of the family, Ric Somervell, brought a great many complications into the situation—and into Cherry's life!

STORMY RAPTURE
by Margaret Pargeter
Liza Lawson and her mother considered that they had been treated shabbily by old Silas Redford. It seemed outrageous that he should have left all he possessed not to them, but to some nephew whom he had never even known. And things became even more difficult when Simon Redford turned up to claim his inheritance . . .

DEAR VILLAIN
by Jacqueline Gilbert
Liz was looking forward immensely to her new job as deputy stage manager at the splendid new Queensbridge Civic Theatre—until she learned that the director was going to be Adam Carlyon. For Adam Carlyon was a man she had no wish whatsoever to meet again . . .

DAMSEL IN GREEN
by Betty Neels
It was chance that Nurse "George" Rodman was on duty when the van den Berg Eyffert children came into hospital after the accident and chance that their guardian, Professor van den Berg Eyffert, was staying near George's home in Essex, which got her the job of going to Holland. He was able to arrange with Matron to have George "on loan" for a reasonable time. But soon George found herself wishing that she could be there "for keeps".

30p net each
Available April 1976

Look out for eight splendid doctor-nurse romances – available April 16th

CHILDREN'S HOSPITAL
by Elizabeth Gilzean
Would Sister Sandra Lorraine and 'new broom' consultant Peter Donaldson ever come to understand each other?

HOSPITAL CORRIDORS
by Mary Burchell
Madeline was looking forward to her year in a big Montreal hospital. Would she be disappointed?

DOCTOR LUCY
by Barbara Allen
Lucy was through with love and intended to concentrate on her career—as she made clear to her chief, that clever surgeon Paul Brandon.

BORNE ON THE WIND
by Marjorie Moore
Why was Duncan McRey so kind to his child patients and yet so harsh and unfriendly to Sister Jill Fernley?

A PROBLEM FOR DOCTOR BRETT
by Marjorie Norrell
Brett Hardy had two things to do before leaving St. Luke's Hospital—apologise to Sister Janet Morley, and then consult a marriage bureau ...

SUCH FRAIL ARMOUR
by Jane Arbor
Kathryn could have borne Adam Brand's hostility if she hadn't had to work alongside him all day and every day!

JUNGLE HOSPITAL
by Juliet Shore
A romantic story set in the jungle of Malaya.

THE HEART OF A HOSPITAL
by Anne Vinton
Would Sister Eve Ramsey's selfish sister manage to ruin her career?

Available April 1976

35p net each

Free! Your copy of the Mills & Boon Catalogue –'Happy Reading'

If you enjoyed reading this Mills & Boon romance and would like to obtain details of other Mills & Boon romances which are available, or if you're having difficulty in getting your ten monthly Mills & Boon romances from your local bookshop, why not drop us a line and you will receive, by return and post free, the Mills & Boon catalogue—'Happy Reading'.

Not only does it list nearly 400 Mills & Boon romances, but it also features details of all future publications and special offers.

For those of you who can't wait to receive our catalogue we have listed over the page a selection of current titles. This list may include titles you have missed or had difficulty in obtaining from your usual stockist. Just tick your selection, fill in the coupon below and send the whole page to us with your remittance including postage and packing. We will despatch your order to you by return!

MILLS & BOON READER SERVICE, P.O. BOX 236, 14 Sanderstead Road, South Croydon, Surrey CR2 0YG, England.

Please send me the free Mills & Boon catalogue ☐
Please send me the titles ticked ☐

I enclose £.....................(No C.O.D.) Please add 5p per book— standard charge of 25p per order when you order five or more paperbacks. (15p per paperback if you live outside the UK).

Name ....

Address ....

City/Town ....

County/Country.....................Postal/Zip Code..............................

*Will S. African & Rhodesian readers please write to:—

    P.O. BOX 11190
    JOHANNESBURG, 2000
    S. AFRICA

NEW TITLES ONLY are available from this address.
MB 3/76

Your Mills & Boon Selection!

- [ ] 002
  MY TENDER FURY
  Margaret Malcolm
- [ ] 007
  THE THIRD UNCLE
  Sara Seale
- [ ] 133
  INHERIT MY HEART
  Mary Burchell
- [ ] 203
  KINGFISHER TIDE
  Jane Arbor
- [ ] 255
  PARADISE ISLAND
  Hilary Wilde
- [ ] 293
  HOTEL BY THE LOCH
  Iris Danbury
- [ ] 307
  THE DREAM AND THE
  DANCER
  Eleanor Farnes
- [ ] 336
  PEPPERCORN HARVEST
  Ivy Ferrari
- [ ] 927
  WITCHSTONE
  Anne Mather
- [ ] 935
  THE SNOW ON THE HILLS
  Mary Wibberley
- [ ] 944
  SWEET ROOTS AND HONEY
  Gwen Westwood
- [ ] 950
  DANGEROUS TO KNOW
  Elizabeth Ashton

- [ ] 957
  DARLING JENNY
  Janet Dailey
- [ ] 962
  AUTUMN CONCERTO
  Rebecca Stratton
- [ ] 967
  HEAVEN IS GENTLE
  Betty Neels
- [ ] 972
  THE SMOKE AND THE FIRE
  Essie Summers
- [ ] 977
  RETURN TO DEEPWATER
  Lucy Gillen
- [ ] 982
  NO ORCHIDS BY REQUEST
  Essie Summers
- [ ] 987
  A PAVEMENT OF PEARL
  Iris Danbury
- [ ] 993
  FIRE AND ICE
  Janet Dailey
- [ ] 1003
  THE FARAWAY BRIDE
  Linden Grierson
- [ ] 1008
  RIDE OUT THE STORM
  Jane Donnelly
- [ ] 1013
  THE WIDE FIELDS OF HOME
  Jane Arbor
- [ ] 1017
  WESTHAMPTON ROYAL
  Sheila Douglas

All priced at 25p. Please tick your selection and use the
handy order form supplied overleaf.